The Crooked Lake Chronicles

The Crooked Lake Chronicles

Mostly True Stories of Life Up North

Mike Lein

Jackpine Writers' Bloc, Inc.
Menahga, Minnesota 56464

Some of the chapters in this book have appeared in edited
forms in other publications as noted below.

Lake Country Journal Magazine: a version of "Crooked Lake
Chowder."

Muzzleloader Magazine: a version of "Winter Grouse."

Talking Stick: "Someday," "Strange Barn Fellows."

All illustrations and cover artwork contributed
by Erik Espeland.

Acknowledgments

The Crooked Lake Chronicles is the third book of what I am calling "The Cabin Trilogy." *Firewood Happens* and *Down at the Dock* are my earlier two books which make up the "series of three" and the "single theme" needed for a trilogy. While not every story is set at our family cabin, a simple lifestyle and good people are what ties these stories together. The cabin needs no acknowledgment. However, these books could not have been written without the good people, neighbors, friends, and some family I have hung out with, met at the cabin, and/or in my travels to other wild, simple places. So, thanks to all—for sharing your stories, your humor, and your hospitality around campfires!

Putting together a series of successful books isn't done by just the writer. Many of the active members of the Jackpine Writers' Bloc deserve credit for being my sounding board and "first draft" editors. They make monthly meetings something to look forward to, meetings where I learn something about my own writing and that of other writers and genres—even poets and poetry. Special thanks are needed for Sharon Harris and Tarah Wolff as content and format editors for the Jackpine Writers' Bloc. My quotation marks and commas would be badly out of place without Sharon and the books would look like some amateur pasted them together without Tarah's knowledge and skills.

The cover and chapter illustrations are the work of Erik Espeland of Field Hands. I don't care how good my writing is, the books would go unnoticed and unsold at many events, gift shops, and book stores if it weren't for Erik's bright cover scenes and the chapter illustrations to grab people's attention and hold it as they flip through pages.

There is also one other group of writers I'd like to acknowledge. Many readers have asked who I look to for inspiration. Others have mentioned how my books and writing style have reminded them of other writers and books. I spent part of the last year pondering these comments and looking back at some of my own favorites. Here's a few that I gratefully acknowledge have influenced my thoughts and writing.

Sigurd F. Olson—Look no farther than his best-selling second book *Listening Point* for one of the best cabin-related books ever written (my humble opinion).

Patrick McManus—You want humor in the outdoors? This guy is the Master. Try *Never Sniff a Gift Fish* for starters.

Sam Cook—Check out his series of books set in northern Minnesota with illustrations by Ely's Bob Cary. *Quiet Magic* is a good place to start.

John J. Rowlands—*Cache Lake Country: Life in the North Woods* is a classic set in the old-time New England Northwoods.

Gordon MacQuarrie—*Stories of the Old Duck Hunters* features hunting, fishing, humor, and companionship in Wisconsin's North Country.

Richard K. Nelson—*The Island Within*. This book details the author's exploration of an island in the Pacific Northwest. One quote has stuck with me since my first read—"There may be more to learn by climbing the same mountain a hundred times than by climbing a hundred different mountains."

Happy Reading!

Table of Contents

The Crooked Lake Chronicles

Chronicles

Mostly True Stories of Life Up North

Spring?

Spring?

    I always feel a sort of nervous anticipation when turning into the cabin's driveway after a long absence. Today is no different, despite having done it for over twenty-five years. Did neighbor Bill remember to plow snow? Will there be a tree down across the driveway, the outhouse, or the cabin? Did I remember the key? With one thousand feet of driveway there's plenty of time to think bad thoughts before making the last turn at the "Labrador Retriever Crossing" sign and seeing the cabin still standing, waiting several hundred feet ahead. No problem there. But it looks like I should have been worrying about the weather, should have checked to see if spring was here.

    Who actually controls the weather in this part of the world? Who tells Mother Nature it's time to switch from one season to another, from winter to spring in this case? Whoever it is needs to get busy and pass on the info. I step out of the truck wearing a winter-warm camouflage coat, the deck thermometer says twenty degrees, and the snow in the woods looks too deep for any travel that doesn't involve snowshoes. How could this happen? After all, the calendar says that the official ground hog looked for his shadow over six weeks ago and that, technically speaking, spring is here.

    Neighbor Bill and his Ford, the mighty "White Stallion" have plowed snow. Lots of snow. There's snow banked up all around the yard, enclosing it like a huge snow fort with barely enough space to park the truck. The banks are taller than me, tall enough to stand on and trim low-hanging trees, tall enough to clean woodduck houses without a ladder. At this rate they might be handy for natural beer refrigeration well into the summer—if summer ever comes.

According to local sources, the lake is still entombed under twenty inches of ice. The dogs and I make a quick trip down the hill to check it out. I have to crunch through drifts at the edge, stumbling out to the wind-swept main lake while black Lab Sage and fluffy, little, white mutt Kaffi scamper on top of the crust. There aren't even any melted spots under the south-facing pine trees where the warmth of the spring sun usually makes its first appearance. There must be an opening somewhere though. Otter tracks and slides are crisscrossing the bay and a beaver is working on a big birch tree on Bird Island. Maybe the beavers use those big buck teeth to cut holes up through the ice when they sense spring is coming.

Back at the cabin there are signs of hope. The half-filled water jugs I left on the last visit didn't freeze solid. The interior thermometer confirms the cabin is just above freezing at thirty-six degrees. It shouldn't take long to heat up once the wood stove gets blazing away. At least it will feel like summer inside.

The bird feeders need to be filled while the wood stove is working up a sustainable blaze. In the dead of winter, the chickadees start dancing and chirping in the empty feeders as soon as the truck is parked. The nuthatches and woodpeckers aren't shy about pointing out the lack of suet and seeds either. Today they are nowhere to be seen. Maybe it's been just warm enough that they have moved on from freeloading and are hunting down their own food. So maybe spring is coming.

I grab the sled and head out to the woodpiles to fill the wood box. The empty stacks behind the outhouse tell their own story. Spring should be here given the amount of firewood that's gone up in smoke. I almost hate to burn more given all the effort that went into scrounging it out of the forest. Some people talk about how many cords of wood they burned each winter, expecting you to do complex math in your head to understand their bragging—or complaining. I just count the number of tarp-covered stacks that have disappeared and how many remain. Five have disappeared, one more than average by my estimations. Five more stacks of hand-split, air-dried, free-range oak still remain. That doesn't count the huge pile of birch that's buried under a mound of snow, unable to be dug out and split over the winter. Maybe I have enough wood for next year despite the long winter. Maybe I can take the summer off from wood-making, if summer ever comes.

Will the snowblower and the ATV start without tinkering? I pump the gas primer bulb on the snowblower and yank the starter rope. It sputters, pops and then catches, rumbling away, echoing out over the lake. I run it around the cabin a few times, clearing a path for firewood hauling and space for the dogs to romp. Maybe it's my lucky day, maybe the ATV will start and take me prospecting for late winter ice fishing spots. I pull the choke out, twist the key and hit the start button. Once again I'm surprised when the noisy little engine comes to life, announcing its readiness to take on the mud. Could it be? Could spring be coming?

The dogs don't seem to care about the season. Both are running amok with toys after the long truck ride. Sage picked out a red-and-orange-striped ball to chase and is tearing up long strips in the mud and dead grass as she slips and slides in pursuit. Kaffi has her precious green squeaky ball and is rapidly turning from fluffy off-white to matted mud as she rolls the toy down snow banks into puddles. Good thing those water jugs in the cabin aren't frozen. There will be plenty of need for water and dog towels until spring comes.

I take a seat on the deck to contemplate life while the dogs continue trashing the yard and themselves. The snow banks around the deck are head-high, blocking the wind off the lake and the sun is peeking around the west corner of the cabin, warming my chair. The twelve-pack left on the railing to cool catches my attention with its bright-colored advertising promising open water, loons, and a dock covered with sunbathers. I bust into it, lean back in the chair to survey my domain and the two muddy dogs at play. Maybe it's a little early for the first deck beer of the year. Then again, it must be five o'clock somewhere. Maybe it's spring there, too.

The Tree

We have tried to cut no tree before its time at our cabin. Most of the trees that were here when we arrived on the scene twenty-five years ago are still standing. The majestic pines I named "The Seven Sisters" provide ambiance to the lakeside fire ring. The driveway slants into the cabin site at an angle purposely planned to miss several mature oaks. The yard is ringed with a mix of aspen, basswood, oak, and birch. Most first-time visitors usually ask—"When are you going to cut down some trees?"

However, there is a time when a tree's time has come. Almost twenty years ago I cut down about half of a small grove of aspens to make way for the cabin. The rest remained, providing shade for the deck and preventing the harsh summer sun from beating down and bleaching the stain on the log siding. In the meantime they grew, something you don't always think about or plan for. They now towered over the cabin and were slowly dying of old age, thin leaves clustered only at their tops, woodpecker holes perforating straight branchless trunks. Two had broken halfway up and crashed down in a wind storm, narrowly missing the truck and the lawn chair Marcie had been reading in only minutes before.

The remaining fifteen or so leaned out over the hillside away from the cabin and would only hurt their brethren when they finally gave up and loosened their grip on the earth. That is, all but one. This was an impressive specimen, about eighteen inches thick and close to one hundred feet tall. It maybe leaned away from the cabin—or maybe not. It was hard to tell given the optical illusion created by the angle of the hillside and tall straight trunk devoid of branches and leaves except for that thin cluster at the top. One thing was clear. It was aging fast and was going to come down one way or the other and in one direction or the other.

So, that tree was going to come down today. There would be no better time. A strong wind was blowing off the lake, pushing the tree away from the cabin and I was by myself. I wanted no witnesses to what was about to happen, no videos posted to social media, no semi-true tales to be embellished by neighbors around future campfires. Call me foolish, irresponsible, or whatever. Either my chainsaw and woodsman's skills were good enough, or they were not. I either was going to celebrate success or start patching a crushed corner of the cabin by myself, with only myself to blame, only myself to swear at.

There is a saying in the Northwoods—"Firewood warms you twice. Once when you split it and once when you burn it." I'm not sure who was the author of that phrase but I would respectfully add to it. "Firewood warms you twice. Once when you split it and once when you burn it. But only if it doesn't kill you first."

I started by clearing brush in a circle around the base of the tree, creating an area where escape in any direction was an option should this project go suddenly awry. Did I mention that the chainsaw started? Clearly a good omen, a sign that the stars were properly aligned today. With the safety zone established, I stepped back and wiped the sweat from my eyes. It was then that I realized how stressful this project had become.

The cool breeze off the lake and the mild temperatures weren't stopping me from breaking out in a cold sweat. My hands gripping the chainsaw were shaking. My heart rate seemed faster than normal. I took a deep breath and planned the next move. I revved the chainsaw, tipped it sideways and started the first cut, a flat slice pointed precisely in the direction I wanted the tree to fall—or hoped it would fall. The saw bit into the rough gray bark and chipped away, seeming to work harder the deeper it got—a good sign that the tree wasn't hollow and even more unpredictable. Halfway through the trunk I stopped, wiped off more sweat, and started a cut six inches above the first, angling down to meet it, and popping out a big wedge from the center of the tree. So far, so good.

The tree stood tall, swaying with the wind gusts, daring me to make the next move. With pounding heart, sweaty palms, and shaking hands, I moved to what hopefully was the backside of the trunk and angled one last cut down to meet the missing wedge. With about two inches left in the cut, the tree surrendered and slowly, ponderously, and unceremoniously thundered down precisely in the direction I had planned. Even better, it narrowly missed both a young maple tree on the left and thick oak on the right.

I took time to consider the deed just done,

measuring the tree and thinking about its history. The stump was nearly twenty inches across. My hundred-foot tape measure ran almost all the way out—eighty-five plus or minus feet tall. I brushed the sawdust off the stump and counted seventy or more growth rings. Some were clustered close together—a sure sign of drought and hard times in the forest. Others were widely spaced from rapid growth in years of plenty. This tree had seen it all.

My work here was just beginning. My chainsaw would burn through many tanks of gas cutting firewood lengths from the downed trunk. My back would ache from carrying them out of the woods, splitting, and stacking them for drying. But first it was time to sit back on the deck to cool down, let my heart stop racing and my hands stop shaking—and to celebrate. I may not be Paul Bunyan's Great Grandson, but damn, I was good today!

Communications

I try to have the outhouse pumped out once a year in the fall, whether it is full or not. After all, winter can be long and cold. There's no sense in being cheap and suddenly finding there's no place to go when I have to go. Lucky for me, there are hardworking folks around here who are willing to do dirty jobs, including pumping outhouses. So I called the guy at the local septic tank pumping service to get it scheduled. He remembered the place.

"You're the guy with the 'Bear Butts Welcome' sign painted on the outhouse door, right?" he asked.

"Yup, that's the one—probably the only one," I replied. "And the bear is still around but he seems to have moved on to destroying bird feeders. He hasn't bothered the outhouse recently. It's unlocked. There's nothing stored in there other than a cheap chainsaw. And if someone steals that, I wish them good luck. Maybe they can figure out how to get it started!"

Most people around here know what you mean when you disparage a cheap chainsaw. He laughed and assured me he wouldn't be tempted. So I headed home confident that one autumn task could be checked off the list. I even made a point of calling my wife Marcie so she would know I was working and not just having fun at the cabin. In hindsight, I should have talked to my father.

Dad showed up at the cabin a day or two later, looking to see if the crappies were biting off the dock. He checked out the outhouse and noticed it was both unlocked and contained a valuable chainsaw. So he locked it, went fishing, and didn't bother to call me. Later that week I did get a call from the septic pumper guy. "Mike, I stopped by to pump your outhouse but it was locked—I couldn't get in."

That was a real head-scratcher. Sure, I had been busy and in a hurry when I left. But I hadn't locked the outhouse—had I? I apologized and assured him it would be unlocked next week. I made the drive to the cabin, got the dock out, raked leaves, mowed the lawn one last time, and made sure the lock on the outhouse was unlatched as I left.

I got another call from the septic guy several days later. "Mike—the outhouse was still locked when I showed up. This time I decided not to waste any more time. I unscrewed the hinges, took the whole door off, and got the job done."

I thanked him for taking the initiative, apologized again, and was once again scratching my head when he hung up. Yeah, you probably guessed the cause. I again forgot to mention this detail to my dad. He had made another appearance at the cabin and again made sure the chainsaw couldn't be stolen from the outhouse. I only figured this out a day or two later when he called to inform me that I was being careless with the outhouse lock—but he was looking out for me.

Communication. It can be such a difficult thing. Especially when people, including me, make assumptions or jump to conclusions. Sometimes there's no damage done and we all get a good laugh. Then again sometimes things spiral out of control and pretty soon there are consequences. Sometimes things die.

I ordered a bunch of crab apple seedlings from the local Soil and Water Conservation District as part of my ongoing grouse habitat-improvement and menu-improvement project. Grouse like to eat crab apples. I like to eat crab apple-fattened grouse. I planted as many as there was time and space for and had half a dozen left. So I called Neighbor One to see if he wanted a few to plant. It seemed like a decent thing to do. We trade seedlings here all the time.

"Sure," he said. "But we aren't home now—won't be back until tomorrow. Just leave them in a bag on the porch and I'll take care of them."

Simple enough. I put the trees into a plastic bag, packed the roots with wet sawdust to prevent drying out, and hiked over to Neighbor One's porch. I even left the original tag on the original bag since it had my name and the type of tree on it. I figured he would know who they came from but might appreciate the name of the variety.

Now things start to get complicated. Neighbor Two showed up on Neighbor One's porch to feed the cats since Neighbor One was gone overnight. He finds a bag with a bunch of trees and my name prominently displayed on the tag. "Aaahh," he thinks. "Some delivery company got the wrong house. I should do the neighborly thing and get them to the right cabin."

So Neighbor Two takes the trees and tries to find my cabin in the somewhat complicated maze of our shared driveways. In his defense, he hadn't been to our cabin before and didn't know that our place is the one with the "Labrador Retriever Crossing" sign. Confused about who's who, but thinking he's right, he leaves the bag of trees on Neighbor Three's porch.

Neighbor Three comes home and finds a bag of trees with my name tag on his porch. He scratches his head and decides that some delivery guy got confused and that the trees must belong at my cabin. Now he knows the neighborhood, so very shortly the bag of trees is back on the deck of Neighbor Four—me. Except that I had headed home and didn't return for over a week. When I did, I was left with the mystery as to how the trees had found their way home and died a slow lingering death as the harsh sun beat down on the deck and dried them to a crisp.

So there you have it. Communication is such a difficult thing when humans are involved. If only outhouses and trees could talk . . .

Signs, Signs, Everywhere There's Signs

WELCOME To OUR NECK OF THE 🌲🌲

Life is Better at the CABIN!

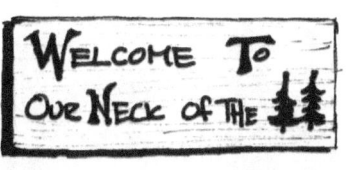

Welcome To THE Lein Cabin

Be Our Guest

Trust me, you can dance.
-Beer

You might think that we lack the signs of civilization here in Cabin Country. By that I'm meaning traffic signs, advertising signs, and the like. We still have our share and, by the way, I happen to believe that folks up here are much more "civilized" than those in some other parts of the country. Official traffic signs may be farther apart but just as professionally done as ones down south. Sometimes the ones advertising a local resort or gift shop are obviously homemade and not by a craftsperson of the sign trade.

Where we make up for numbers of signs is in homes and cabins. I'm willing to bet the number of signs per square foot of dwelling area is ten times that of city dwellers. Let me use my humble cabin as an example. First of all, forget all the signs outside. You know, the classic ones, like "Labrador Retriever Crossing," and "This Way to the Lake." And my favorite: "Welcome To Our Campfire—where both friends and marshmallows get toasted." There's a few more.

Inside, the cabin's four walls have so many that I have to classify them and use examples rather than list them all. I count over thirty and that doesn't include other assorted decorations such as a deer head, two stuffed ducks, a bunch of fake stuffed animals, a trapper's basket . . . Keep in mind our cabin is the size of a small two-car garage.

Attitude. There are several that warn people about bad attitudes, something not allowed at the cabin. "Kwitchurbellyakin," one states—an old Norse phrase that I believe refers to complainers in general and one favored a long time ago by my Aunt Mickey. There's also "No Pouting—if you must, go stand in a corner." No pouting allowed here either although it may be hard to avoid after losing a big fish or expecting a sunny weekend and getting only rain.

Places Visited. My favorite in this category is a small chunk of sanded and varnished log painted with the saying—"Godur er Kaffisopinn." This is an Icelandic saying, roughly translated without the weird apostrophe over the "o," to mean "Coffee is Good." Who's going to argue with that in the morning at the cabin? Keep in mind that wood signs are hard to find in Iceland. They ran out of trees a long time ago. Others in this category include "Wall Drug," a Wisconsin brewery that makes good summer dock-sipping beer, and a yellow painted metal "Fly Alaska" sign with a small float plane. We haven't actually been there yet but it is on the bucket list.

Now we come to the **"Lake Life"** Category—"I'd Rather Be At The Cabin" is an understatement when home and yard maintenance, civic duties and the like force a lengthy stay away from the cabin. Here we also have "Lake Life is Best!" and, of course, "Welcome To The Cabin." Sort of fitting into this category is "Friends Welcome—Relatives by Appointment Only." That one's just a joke. Sort of.

Inspiration. My favorite here is a canoe paddle scribed with a quote from the book *The Singing*

Wilderness written by my favorite cabin author Sigurd F. Olson—"The movement of a canoe is like a reed in the wind. Silence is part of it, and the sounds of lapping water, bird songs, and the wind in the trees. It is part of the medium through which it floats. The sky, the water, the shores. A man is part of his canoe and therefore part of all it knows." Go paddle your canoe and think about that.

Not quite as serious as the above are **Warning Signs**. What cabin would be a cabin without a "Smokey the Bear" sign warning you that "Only You Can Prevent Forest Fires!" Less serious but often true, at least at our place, are "Swim At Your Own Risk—Lifeguard on Beer Break" and "Teach a Man to Hunt And Fish—and you will never see him again." Marcie bought that last one —said it was the truest one she had ever seen. It fits right in with "The Fisherman's Code—Early to Bed. Early to Rise. Fish like Hell and Make up Lies." That's a more traditional different version of "The Code" mentioned elsewhere in this book. Two other warning signs: "Moose Crossing" and "Buffalo Crossing" match up well with the "Labrador Retriever Crossing" one outside on the oak tree.

Food. There's truth to one that states "I forgot to buy food and drinks" in small letters, under big letters proclaiming "Food and Drink." A true statement for many visitors—especially those pesky relatives. Mixed with these are a couple of puns: "Hot Dogs— you'll relish the flavor" and "Hamburgers—stop in and ketchup with the best." Very weak puns in my mind; I didn't buy them.

Two signs proclaim the cabin to be a fine dining

and shopping establishment—"The Blue Heron—Always serving the freshest fish." That's also a weak pun but I don't mind. The second is my current favorite: a Christmas present from the youngest son and fiancé last year—a big round sign shaped like an old fashioned red-and-white fishing bobber painted with the simple words "Bait, Tackle, Ice." It's even weather proof so it can hang over the deck in the summer and set the tone as you walk up to the front door.

These signs, most of which were handmade by northern craftsmen, might have been expensive had we bought them all. However, here's a little-mentioned benefit of having a cabin and sharing it. All the friends, and maybe a few relatives you shared it with, will now shower you with expensive handmade signs as gifts. You might struggle to find room for them if you have a small place like we do. But as I look around the cabin at all these signs, it reminds me that we must have a lot of good friends. And maybe a few good relatives.

Legendary
Freeloaders

One of the fun benefits of being a semi-famous, award-winning Minnesota author is traveling around, talking about cabin life, and telling mostly true tall tales to adoring crowds at libraries, book stores, civic clubs, and the like. I assume they are adoring me and my writing. Then again, it could be the topics, things they are knowledgeable and passionate about. Every crowd is different, so I have developed a few conversation starters designed to get the audience talking about their own experiences. This can be dangerous. You never know what's going to come out of the mouths of babes or passionate adults. Most of the time it's a fun exercise that gets plenty of laughs and generates new material.

One of these conversation starters is the subject of what I will call "Freeloaders" at the cabin. Now let's make it clear, not every friend or relative who visits my cabin or yours is a "Freeloader." There's plenty of good folk out there who are aware of the many stresses cabin ownership can put on the owner—maintenance, mortgage, and taxes, to name a few. Then again, there are some visitors who seem to be clueless about this sort of thing and some of these become what I will call "Legendary Freeloaders." I've even developed three categories of them based on my talks with cabin-loving audiences.

Note that these do not apply to immediate family like sons and daughters. That's a whole other story . . .

Also note that I have had to sanitize some of these experiences for adult language and leave out some details and names to protect the reputations and confidentiality of cabin owners who may have been too candid and passionate about this subject.

First is a very obvious category and probably the biggest by number: "Food and Drink Freeloaders." I am well acquainted with this category because I used to be one. Many years ago, right out of college, a good friend and his wife bought a lake home. We dropped in darn near every weekend, trying to escape from the dull, flat, lake-less town that work had forced Marcie and me to reside in. We didn't think much of it, being young and clueless and fresh out of the college party life scene. We partied on the floating raft, grilled on the deck, and roasted hotdogs around the campfire without much thought to it. Luckily our hosts found a way to tactfully make us aware of it. They started planning a menu of food and drink ahead of time and taking us along shopping for it. Message received. I hope we did better after that.

My audience members almost always come up with an example of Food and Drink Freeloaders that gets all our heads shaking. I don't think many cabin owners expect visitors to show up with a truckload of supplies. But you know, some really good meat for the grill and a cooler of beer will always be noted and appreciated. Don't be like the freeloaders in my current favorite story which was told with numerous "four letter" words. "So," says a cabin owner, "top this! A couple heads north with their three kids to spend a week with us at the cabin. They show up and they have brought an onion for food. Yes, one onion! That's all! They said that they stopped at the Farmers

Market to get some sweet corn but it was sold out. So they bought an onion. One onion!"

Next let's talk about visitors who don't seem to realize that lawns don't mow themselves at the cabin. Buildings don't paint themselves. Firewood does not magically appear in the dark of the night as a gift from firewood elves. All this stuff takes work—work that often has to be done on weekends and vacations before the cabin owners themselves can go fishing, have a beer on the deck, or take a dip in the lake. Now I admit this has happened to me in sort of a reverse way. I've often used the excuse of "having company" to dodge work assignments at our own cabin when the harder-working neighbors and/or my wife ask me why the dock isn't in yet or a landscaping project is taking a while to complete.

The best example of this type of freeloading visitor came from another event. A guy related how a family of visitors (they might have been semi-relatives) came for a weekend stay. The cabin owner labored late into Saturday afternoon on a hot August day—mowing lawn and taking care of other routine tasks. The visitors played in the lake, enjoyed his dock, burned his boat gas, and had themselves a real good time. He finally completed his task list and took to the lake himself to cool off, have a drink, and relax. It was not to be. The visitors, having exhausted themselves and the boat gas, retreated to the cabin deck and complained about being hungry. That did not sit well. More "four letter words" were spoken . . .

The third and final category deals with those visitors who overstay their welcome. I'm not sure I have a good example of myself being in this category, unless it was all those days and nights we spent at my parents' lake home back in the day. But that's different—we're family, after all, and the parents really wanted to spend time with the grandkids and the granddogs. Right? Anyway, think about this. Maybe you brought a whole food and drink meal plan to a friend's cabin—the good stuff even. Things like steaks and bacon from the local award-winning meat market and craft beer and a few bottles of wine from local sources. And you helped mow the lawn and move some landscaping rocks around. Great. Now how long do you plan on staying?

An extreme example of this comes from one of my adoring fans who related this story from his childhood. He and his parents went to the lake cabin for a typical weekend visit, expecting a short stay filled with family activities. On Saturday morning, an acquaintance and his family stopped by and asked a difficult question—"We were in the area and remembered you said that we were welcome to stop in any time. Would you mind if we stayed overnight?"

Well, what's the typical Minnesota Nice cabin owner going to say to that? We all know the answer is "Okay." And that the owner and his family will rearrange their activities, and perhaps the sleeping arrangements in the cabin, to make sure the visitors have a good stay. Then came the next day, Sunday afternoon. The owners were cleaning up, packing up, putting the boat up on the lift, and all that when the Head Visitor approached. "We've got the whole week off. Would you mind if we stayed 'a few' more days?"

So, what's the typical Minnesota Nice cabin owner supposed to say to that? The answer in this case is that the owners never did know how long the visitors stayed. It might have been two days or two weeks since their own busy schedule prevented them from returning for a few weeks. Speculation on the length of stay and what happened during it have become part of their cabin lore—something that still comes up around the campfire on summer nights.

Which brings us to the term "Legendary Freeloaders" and some advice for all those potential cabin visitors out there. You don't want to become one of the visitors that are the stuff legends are made of. Someone that tales are told about around the cabin's campfire ring. Tales that start like—"Do you remember when those people from work showed up a few years ago? The ones with the two puppies that weren't housetrained and the kid who was afraid of the dark and would start crying every time a loon wailed? Man, could they eat and drink! I don't think they even brought so much as an onion for food. And the guy claimed he had never run a lawnmower! Did they stay two days or two weeks?"

Perhaps the best advice I can give to potential visitors based on my surveys of cabin owners can be summed up by reworking an old saying attributed to Benjamin Franklin and a few even earlier wise old men —"Fish, and visitors who don't bring food and drink, don't help mow the lawn, and who stay more than three days, stink."

Out Of Sync

Many cabin activities have a rhythm, often driven by Mother Nature and the flow of the seasons. Ice fishing in winter. Turkey hunting and crappie fishing in spring. Trolling for northern pike and swimming in the summer. Duck, grouse, and deer hunting in the fall. Of course there are other less fun things that need to be accomplished with the seasons. Putting up firewood is one that tends to span them all.

Summer brings morning excursions into the forest to collect leftovers from logging operations, working early and at a leisurely pace to avoid the heat and bugs. During the fall, big logs get chainsawed into stove-length pieces for splitting in the cold winter, while woodsmoke from the chimney assures me warmth and comfort is waiting inside. Spring is a time to consolidate firewood leftovers and consider next year's needs.

Sometimes spring doesn't come when it's supposed to. It was mid-May by the time the tarp could be pulled off the pile of unsawed birch logs, logs that should have been chainsawed over winter but had spent six months buried under snow. I poked at the edge of the pile and found a sign of how far out of sync my firewood process had become.

Peeking out of the sawdust under a birch log were five inches of delicate blue spotted salamander. I never realized or thought much about salamanders in the past. The only ones I knew of were the big orange spotted ones that showed up in window wells in the fall. Then years ago, early in the process of clearing the building site, I turned over a rotting log and found a new one, about five inches long, coal black, shiny with moisture and dotted with bright fluorescent blue spots. I took a picture, carefully placed it under another log out of the flow of traffic, and searched for "blue spotted salamander" when I got home to internet access. Some unknown scientist had named a creature for what it looked like—a blue spotted salamander. While endangered in some parts, I have since found them to be common in our neck of the woods, especially in early summer during wet periods.

During last spring's inventory, I appeared to have an ample supply of high quality oak already split and stacked. Pickings in the forest had been easy the year before. But firewood collecting can be addicting and supply concerns have a way of staying active in the back corners of your brain, nagging at you, leading to doubts and thoughts that maybe too much is never enough. Come summer, a section of forest just across the road was logged. Several piles of birch logs beckoned, so close they could be heard calling from the deck of the cabin, like a beer in the basement fridge on a hot day. I relented, stopped in at the local forestry office for a permit, and went to work.

The pile of unsawed logs next to the outhouse grew load by load as I sawed birch into six-foot lengths and hauled them back to the cabin on the utility trailer. I quit hauling several times, thinking the pile was large enough. Yet I could still hear the remains of the wood calling, just a quarter of a mile away, across the road, waiting. I'd relent and go get just one more load, a process that repeated itself until there was no more room to stack.

Summer progressed into fall. In between hunting excursions and getting the dock and swim raft out, I pulled the chainsaw from the outhouse and attacked the front of the pile one tank of gas at a time, zipping logs into foot and a half lengths and tossing them to the back of the pile. It was a good year for hunting excursions. I was only halfway through the pile when winter arrived and the mixed pile of sawed and unsawed logs had to be covered with a big blue tarp before snow mixed in and froze everything into one icy lump.

I have a system for splitting wood in the winter. Anytime I'm near the outhouse and the surrounding storage area, whether it be to start the ATV or attend to other business, I split a few rounds and stack them. Like the process of gathering firewood from the forest, this can be an addictive behavior. It's good honest work that gets me out of the snowbound cabin and sends me tripping down memory lane, reminiscing about former good jobs and bad. Like the unpleasant heat, humidity, and back-breaking labor associated with baling hay back on the farm. Or the more pleasant task of cleaning a bucket of crappies by lantern light while sharing a beer with fishing buddies. Before you know it, the woodpile is smaller and the firewood stacks are larger.

It's also a task that requires a certain level of experience and knowledge. Every log has its differences. A chainsaw cut here or there will influence how easy the chunks break apart once the splitting maul slams down. A knot or a fork left in the middle of a piece can spell trouble then and that trouble is best avoided by careful use of the chainsaw. Each piece also has a unique character best sized up once placed on the splitting block. Careful consideration will have the maul working with existing cracks, with the grain instead of against it, and limiting the lifting and swinging by aging arms and shoulders.

This winter had other ideas. It decided that I had gotten complacent about the wimpy amounts of snow the last few winters had brought. While I scratched my ice fishing itch out on the lake and nailed down knotty pine in the cabin, snow piled up, on, and around the firewood and kept coming. Bill, the Snow Plow Neighbor, was able to handle the driveway and yard with his mighty Ford, but the snow had to go somewhere. Soon the woodpile was buried—an unrecognizable mound under many feet of both natural and plowed snow next to the outhouse. Warm and comfortable in the cabin, I passed on shoveling out the pile.

So here I was. I had gambled on the weather and lost and now was getting a nature lesson. I took this salamander to a safe new home back in the woods in another log pile. I then returned to the woodpile, pulled the chainsaw from the outhouse where it was stored, and gassed it up. I can take a hint. When your woodpile has become habitat for strange little creatures, you know it's time to get busy.

The Gift of Firewood

There's all kinds of gifts associated with life at the cabin. Small gifts, like slipping the granddaughter a crisp five-dollar bill for an ice cream cone on the long drive home from the cabin on Sunday afternoon. Bigger gifts, like a bottle of medium shelf wine presented to the host of a lakeside Memorial Day cookout. And big gifts, like the new pontoon the kids have always wanted for lake fun. Or that really big gift of passing ownership of the family cabin on to the next generation.

Of these, one gift is always appropriate at our place. It's not uncommon at our nightly campfires to have a neighbor call a greeting from the darkness and walk into the glow of the campfire bearing an armload of firewood for a gift. Now this may seem fitting of that saying about bringing "coals to Newcastle" or even the one about selling ice cubes to the residents of the frozen Arctic. Not here. We understand and welcome this gift, even though the neighbor may have walked past the many tarped stacks of firewood we have available.

The neighbor knows that the wood warming our gathering was the product of sweaty labor and maybe even some blood and tears. Nobody in this neighborhood buys firewood delivered, cut, split, stacked, and dried. We forage from the forest or from our own trees. Trees that might be in the way of a building project or have died a natural death due to old age or bugs. There was honest sweat and effort put into the firewood-making process. There might even have been blood if a chainsaw went awry or a splitting maul missed its mark. There might have been tears had the tree been a favorite, an old soul shading the deck or providing a convenient resting spot on the trek uphill from the lake. Likewise the campfire host knows that the neighbor bearing the gift went through the same process. It's not a gift to be given or taken lightly.

Sometimes firewood is a perfect gift even if you don't know the gifter. Picture if you will, pulling into the perfect campsite on the yearly family vacation at a state park or other public camping area. The kids are restless and crabby from the long ride. You are restless and crabby from the long drive and the nagging worry that a trailer tire will blow or the truck transmission might overheat. But there it is, the perfect campsite. Included are a big open flat spot to pitch the tent or park the trailer. Big trees for shade even in the hottest part of the day. A buffer of trees and brush screening your site from others. A big picnic table setting next to a campfire. To top it off, there, alongside the fire ring, is a big stack of firewood, ready for your first night in paradise. Some unknown camper has paid it forward with a gift of firewood to you and your family.

We've been the recipients of firewood gifts many times in our travels. Maybe Marcie, the dogs, and I look lonely and needy when we are camping alone. Or maybe the friendly dogs struck a note with someone who is missing their own pets. Or maybe we were on a family trip and the granddaughter's new vacation friends had to leave early and gifted us their leftover firewood. In any case, we often return to the campsite from a fishing excursion to find our once meager supply of wood has grown like the loaves and fishes in that bible story. It's these people who give you hope for humanity and who we hope have a very special place waiting for them in the hereafter.

Of course there are a few scrooges out there, people who were probably cattle rustlers in the Old West in another lifetime. Once, and only once, I crossed paths with one. I was on a solo camping trip in the far north, near the Boundary Waters Canoe Area. I stopped at the park office and purchased two bundles of DNR-approved, shrink-wrapped firewood for my night's entertainment. Being the connoisseur of fine firewood that I am, the bundles were carefully selected from the pile, ensuring that each had some birch to get the fire going and some oak to keep the fire burning long into the night.

I then drove to that perfect campsite mentioned earlier. No one had gifted me firewood yet. No problem. I had those two carefully selected shrink-wrapped bundles of prime northern Minnesota DNR-approved birch and oak. I took them off the truck's tailgate, put them on the picnic table, and drove off to the boat landing to launch the boat. When I returned, the firewood was gone—vanished in less than fifteen minutes.

Now it could have been Sasquatch, I suppose, looking for a little entertainment and comfort in whatever place Sasquatch lives. But I'm pretty sure it was another camper—an opportunist who would snatch

that five-dollar bill from your granddaughter's hand
or walk away from a party with an unopened bottle of
the host's gifted wine. I don't suppose we can resort
to capital punishment for these lowdown types when
caught. But I hope there is a special place for
firewood rustlers, a very special place, a very
special warm place in the hereafter.

Ice Holes I have Known—A Short History of Ice Fishing

Ice fishing used to be such a simple sport. Way back then we would take an old fishing pole, a bucket, and a hatchet and take a long walk out to a frozen lake. A spot on the icy featureless surface would be chosen based on warm summer memories floating in a boat. The hatchet would be used to hack a hole through the ice while scooping ice chips with a bare, soon-to-be-frozen hand. The last few chops were the worst—icy water splashing in the face while trying to widen the hole as water rushed in.

Next came the wait. Sit on the overturned bucket for an hour or two, staring at an unmoving bobber while the wind whipped across the lake, blew up the back of your jacket, and turned your butt into a frozen piece of meat. If the fish didn't bite, and they rarely did, moving was not a logical option. Who would want to hack another hole through three feet of ice with a dull hatchet after they had done it once? I said ice fishing was simple then. I didn't say it was easy, productive, or fun.

Hard water fishing got a little more complicated and much more fun when I got older. One of the benefits of attending college in northern Minnesota was the proximity of a lake right outside the door of the dorm. It was there a friend introduced me to dark house spearing, a weird Midwestern version of ice fishing. The friend had a small, homemade ice fishing house, different from the few I had seen in the past.

47

It had a two-foot by three-foot hole in the floor and no windows. In this cozy unheated structure, you sat on a bucket, in the dark, staring down the large hole with a four-pronged spear close at hand.

It was like staring into a vast wild aquarium. The lack of ambient light inside, coupled with the bright winter sunshine outside, allowed you to see down through over ten feet of clear northern lake water. A weighted wood or plastic minnow-shaped fish decoy hung below, attached to a length of fish line. Give the line a twitch and the decoy would swim out and away like a paper airplane and glide back to hover below. Schools of small perch, fast little fish with gold skin and black stripes, would rush to the decoy and peck at it, curious over this strange intruder. If you were lucky, a big northern pike, with its white spots gleaming on brilliant green skin, would glide in below your feet to look at the decoy, trying to decide if it was edible. If you were real lucky, the spear was pushed, not thrown, down the hole, impaling the unlucky fish. Then came a rush of activity as the thrashing pike was swung out of the hole, slime and blood flying around the tight confines, while being shoved out the door into the natural freezer of the cold northern air.

I spent my first Christmas vacation back home building a portable spear house and then trekking it back north in the trunk of my parents' car. Now I had a sport to pursue on the long winter days when I didn't feel like attending class or studying and on the weekends when other classmates where sleeping off the previous night's party. It also was a useful sport come Sunday evening when the college food service wasn't open. I would walk out to the fish house, chisel open the hole through sometimes three feet of ice, and hope that my evening meal would swim in to look at the decoy. You weren't supposed to cook in the dorm rooms, but an elicit toaster oven broiled up fresh northern pike for me and roommates on many occasions.

We weren't supposed to drink then either. So the fish house provided a safe haven from the prying eyes of the authorities on a few occasions. Some of my acquaintances even claimed they used the unlocked house to rendezvous with girlfriends. I personally chalk those stories up to pre-adult bravado. Not that many of us actually had girlfriends and it's hard to imagine anything too romantic happening in a four-foot-square unheated fish house at thirty below zero.

This little haven proved to be a bit too portable in the end. Someone folded it up in the dark of some winter night and probably stuffed it into the trunk of their car. I never saw it again and for a time moved on to other sports like grouse hunting, beer drinking, and the pursuit of some romance in my own life.

Today ice fishing has taken on new life at the cabin. While I wouldn't rate Crooked Lake as an ice fishing hotspot, there are enough crappies and northern pike to make it interesting with the aid of a big pile of modern sporting equipment. I reflected on these while heading out for a recent expedition onto a foot and a half of frozen water.

There's no long walk to a suspected hotspot. That's nice. But will the old ATV start so that I can ride to a known fishing hole guided by my GPS? No more ice-hacking hatchet either. Just a heavy, loud, gas-powered ice auger that will spin through the foot and a half of ice in five seconds—if it starts. The old bucket seat and homemade ice house have been replaced with a fold-up portable ice house complete with padded bench seat and a gas heater. The old fishing pole has been left behind for a zipped case packed with three ice fishing rods and a host of lures. Add in the small backpack full of snacks and an insulated minnow bucket containing a swarm of crappie minnows. Did I mention the insulated bib overalls and coat complete with flotation to save me from an icy death should I hit a weak spot? Where did all this stuff come from?

The ATV starts this time so off we go, over the snow, through the woods, and out onto the lake. I stop when landmarks and the GPS indicate we have arrived at tonight's potential hotspot. I confidently drill two holes, use the ATV's snow plow to clear away the snow and pop the ice house up over the holes. Next I fire up the space heater, drop a line down a hole, and adjust the fish finder. No fish are showing on the glowing screen of the electronic gizmo. The wily silver-sided crappies will likely wait until sundown to use their big gold eyes to zero in on unsuspecting smaller fish in the fading light. I dig some trail mix and jerky out of the pack and dig deeper for the beer.

Dang. I didn't just forget an opener this time; I forgot the BEER . . .

It's a long ride back across the lake, over the

snow and through the woods to the cabin's beer fridge. Is it worth the time and the grief I will get from my loving wife, who will likely ask "What did you forget this time?" as I sneak in the basement door? Decision-making time is delayed as I hear good old neighbor Marv approaching on his ATV. I unzip the fish house to greet him.

"Any fish yet?" he yells over the rattle of the motor.

"Nope," I yell. "I just started and I have a big problem—forgot my beer!"

"No problem," he yells back and spins his ATV around on the ice for the short trip back to his cabin. He's back in less than five minutes and hands two cans through the door. "Hope you don't mind drinking this stuff."

It's not my brand but desperate times call for desperate measures. "It will do just fine," I answer. "Now all I need is the fish to bite."

Marv heads over to his cozy little shack, shuts down the ATV, and disappears inside. Silence reigns over the lake again, nothing but the faint hum of the fish finder spinning away, waiting to display hungry fish. I settle back in the warm padded seat and reflect on how enjoyable ice fishing has become over the years. Sure, it's not as simple as it once was and there still are no guarantees that the fish will bite. But, I'm warm and comfortable and I have a neighbor who delivers.

Sucker Fishing

It's impossible to name all the types of fish that swim in lakes up here. We got your walleyes for the walleye fisherperson who likes to waste days dragging leeches and night crawlers for a very few tasty fillets. We got your northern pike for fisherpeople like me who just love to troll an old red-and-white spoon or shiny silver Rapala in hopes of a vicious attack by a toothy predator. We got your sunnies and crappies to keep the fisherkids down on the dock squealing at the sight of a bobber going down. I could go on and name a host of other fish and fishermen. Let's stop there and talk about one more: the lowly and not-often-talked-about sucker fish and sucker fishermen.

The sucker is often regarded as a lowly bottom feeder, full of bones and tasting remarkably like the bottom of a muddy lake. There's quite a few different species of sucker, usually with some sort of color in their name—white sucker, blue sucker, golden redhorse sucker. You get the picture. Most fisherpeople disdain them as a sporting fish and consider them not fit for human consumption unless something drastic is done to the flesh. Pickling it for weeks or soaking in a spicy brine and smoking to the consistency of a scaly jerky are the preferred methods.

However there are sucker fishermen—guys who do target them. The suckers swim upstream from lakes in the early spring to spawn before the regular fishing season and offer up a chance to do something related to fishing while waiting for the big day. You might see these men standing on the banks of a stream with a spear in hand or soaking worms on the bottom of a river pool while enjoying a campfire and a twelve-pack.

Now we come to another type of sucker fisherman. You will notice I switched to masculine words as soon as I started talking about suckers. That's because I have yet to see a fisherwoman engage in what I am about to describe. It may be due to a smaller sense of adventure or maybe just that they have more sense. You see, the sucker fishermen I'm talking about now don't actually target sucker fish. They are suckers who fish, "suckers" as defined by the dictionary as "someone who is easily deceived or drawn in."

Now I'm not talking here about the guys who are "suckered in" by the latest shiny fishing lure, electronic gizmo with bright colored lights, or flashy boat. These guys are drawn to the small, usually unpopulated scenic lakes that hide in the deep dark forest. Some of these lakes have unimproved roads nearby, allowing brief beckoning glimpses of pristine water. Others only show on maps or aerial photos. They all bring the same sense of wonder to the type of sucker fisherman I'm talking about.

Do they contain trophy fish? Are they a secret fishing hole, just waiting to be found and enjoyed by me—and only me—while the hordes of other fisherpeople fight each other at the boat launches and prime fishing spots on well-known lakes?

In my experience, these thoughts lead to

actions, actions that usually involve trekking through mosquito-infested and deerfly-infested thorny underbrush to reach the shore of a hidden potential hotspot. Or packing a canoe, kayak, or some other sort of lightweight watercraft through the same buggy, thorny underbrush, on the hottest, muggiest day of the year, sweating and swearing as that lightweight watercraft gains weight and catches on the thorny underbrush with every hard-fought step. Ninety-nine percent of the time the results are the same. The shore of the pristine lake turns out to be a muddy bog holding nothing but more bugs and now blood-sucking leeches that attach themselves to your various extremities in the struggle to reach open fishless water.

I feel for these guys. I'm one of them. I've had many of these experiences, yet still fall prey to this strange desire to find an untouched spot with fish jumping up to meet my fishing lure on every cast. There's always hope and sometimes there's a new twist.

A little lake off a forest road beckoned to me for years as I resisted its siren song and tried to ignore its charms. Then I got a hot tip. A trusted local source slipped up one day, violated The Fisherman's Code, and mentioned the lake did indeed contain walleyes. As mentioned before, I tend to ignore walleyes. Sure, they are the Minnesota State Fish and they taste pretty good. But the hour-per-fish ratio is pretty poor and the sometimes restrictive regulations most often send me looking for fun fish like crappies, sunnies, and northerns. Could this local info be true? I came up with a plan, a low effort plan.

Rather than try to access the lake via the usual bug-infested, thorny brush, blood-sucker method, I waited for December and the first six inches of ice on this little gem of a lake. Brother-in-law Dale, his son Chad, and I parked on the forest road and used the frozen surface of an interconnected swamp as a winter highway to the lake. It was a long trudge, through falling snow and below freezing temperatures, pulling sleds full of gear. It sure beat the hell out of the bugs, thorns, leeches, and heat of summer.

We drilled a few holes, something like fifty or so, and found a deep spot that held promise. Here we made our play, breaking out fish finders, tip-ups and squirming minnows, hoping we had found the Promised Land.

No fish showed on our high-tech fish finders. No tip-up flags swung up and waved in the stiff breeze. No bobbers bobbed. The snow fell harder. The wind blew more. We drilled more holes and fished on in solitude, still hopeful our local info would prove good.

Late into the afternoon, I heard the whine of several approaching snowmobiles following our tracks through the swamp. Pretty soon a pack of a half-dozen came into sight, zooming across the lake for the trail on the other side. One bright yellow machine split from the pack, whined over, and stopped near me. The rider shut it down, dismounted, and removed his helmet. "Is that you, Mike?" he asked. "How are they biting?"

The voice and helmetless face were now recognizable: a trusted guy who lives on a nearby lake and does a lot of fishing.

"Hey, Terry—didn't recognize you with the new snowmobile. Nothing yet but I've heard there are some walleyes in here."

"Well, there were," he responded. "But I know a bunch of local guys hit it pretty hard this summer. I'm pretty sure they fished them out. Good luck—I got to catch up to the other guys."

He zoomed off in pursuit of his friends, leaving three ice fishermen with deflated dreams in his snow dust. We fished on. After all, we were here and maybe one or two were left swimming yet. I stared down my ice hole hoping to see something swim by. It wasn't to be. As darkness approached, not a fish was seen, not even a sucker. Except for the gray-haired bearded one staring back up at me from the refection on the still water in the ice hole.

The Fisherman's Code

A sort-of niece-in-law on a nearby lake took to social media recently, bragging about her and her daughter's success fishing for crappies and perch without a man along in the boat. Pictures and the name of the lake were included. Now this may seem like a gross violation of the first rule of "The Fisherperson's Code"—"NEVER give up the location of a fishing hotspot to the public." But Rhondie was smarter than that. She knows it's a big lake with plenty of fishing spots to confuse people with. So she used another part of The Code—code names. When asked about the spot, she replied, "Across the lake from the skinny dippers' beach, north of the grumpy pontoon guy's dock." I'm in on The Code and knew right where to head the next night.

I'm not sure a full version of The Fisherperson's Code has ever been reduced to written form. However, this is a good example of the concept and the use of it. The extended family and I have fished this lake for over thirty years and have stories about locations that only we might be in on. The grumpy pontoon guy's dock for example. This guy seems to think he owns the whole lake and isn't afraid to yell at people fishing in front of his dock. We might honor his wishes if he's around but do take his name in vain around the campfire. We also might take a few of "his" fish when he's gone on weekends.

The "skinny dippers'" dock refers to an evening

when not only the mosquitoes and crappies came out to play. A young athletic buck-naked couple took multiple runs down a dock at sunset, holding hands, jumping high and splashing down. Now, skinny dipping with a close friend is not that uncommon in the North Country. But this couple was apparently both naked and not afraid. We were anchored just offshore and a crowd of maybe ten onlookers stood on shore with camera flashes blinking, recording the event. Those of us fishing nearby were left wondering. Lost a high stakes bet? Non-traditional engagement photo? Just plain drunk? Whatever the reason, if you were there that night, you remember the spot.

On my own lake, docks are fewer and farther between, so we have modified The Code to include more natural features. "Road Runner Island" refers to an island that creative minds might say is shaped like a bird when viewed from outer space. In fact, it looks like the cartoon character "Road Runner" minus the pursuing "Wile E. Coyote." A casual visitor floating in the lake wouldn't know which one of the many islands it is and might not even know about Road Runner, Wile E. Coyote, and ACME Tools and Bomb Supply. That's knowledge we've kept to ourselves. Well, at least until now.

Here's another example. "Stony Point" might sound self-explanatory. However, those of us dwelling on the lake know there's only one real "Stony Point" amid the many rocky points of Crooked Lake. I better leave readers to figure out that one on their own lest I get accused of another violation of The Code.

Another good way to protect fishing spots is the

use of multiple features. My sort-of niece used a simple version of that in the beginning. After all, many people on her lake might have gotten yelled at by the grumpy pontoon guy and can figure that out. But there were only a few of us on the lake the night of the skinny dipping episode, so only us fortunate souls can zero in on where those big crappies were hanging out.

Sometimes you have to get really creative. Say I'm asked in a public place or forum about a good spot on Crooked Lake. Don't kid yourself. Whether it be while having breakfast at the local café or answering a post on social media, there are ears listening and eyes watching, waiting for a known expert fisherman like myself to give up a hotspot.

Now I wouldn't want to act dumb, selfish, or admit to not catching much. I have a reputation to uphold. So I might rattle off something like "There's some crappies biting at the usual time in front of the birch clump down the shore from the leaning tree in the small bay."

Try to find that if you aren't in on The Code. There's lots of trees leaning over the water on Crooked Lake. Lots of birch clumps. Lots of small bays. And maybe the usual time is dawn, noon, dusk, or dark. But if you know the lake and, if you know The Code, you know where to go.

So think hard the next time you are asked to give up a hotspot. Work out The Code beforehand with your trusted fishing partners. Use multiple references —practice the same type of security as you would for the password to your bank account or online dating account. And finally, try throwing in some decoys or diversions, examples that will change the conversation away from fishing so that lurking ears and eyes will forget about fishing altogether. Trust me. Most people are going to want to know more about skinny dipping in front of a crowd than a hot fishing spot.

The Big Boat

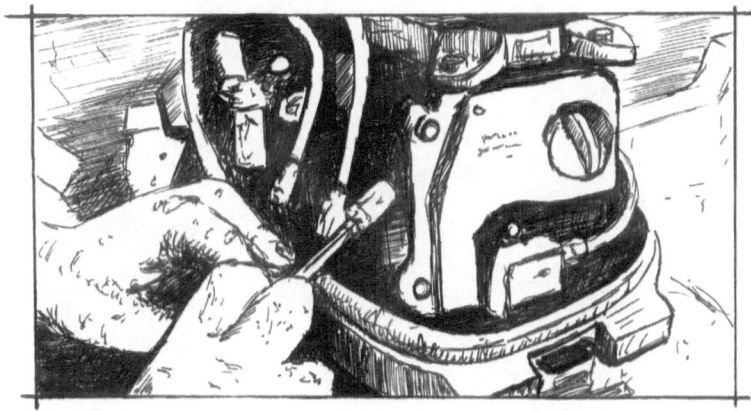

My dad bought the first family boat a little more than a half century ago, after he turned from a life of farming to that of a small town insurance agent and now supposedly had time to use a boat. The purchase involved a long drive from Southwest Minnesota, where there was apparently a shortage of used boats, to the Cities. After some tense negotiations with the seller, he and I proudly towed home a red-and-white fiberglass Larson with a 35-horse Mercury hanging off the stern. We had our first "Big Boat." It wasn't a luxury cruiser fit for Minnetonka but was big enough for us common folk used to renting row boats at resorts on short vacations.

My dad's boats got bigger over the years. Sometimes too big. Imagine sitting on the deck of my parent's lake home, looking out over the glassy water on a perfect early evening. Dad says, "Looks like a nice night. Anyone want to go for a boat ride?"

The answer seems easy until the details are considered. The current Larson, a huge strange pinkish orange-and-white fiberglass runabout with a big round motor of questionable age and manufacture, is perched on the boatlift that a local farmer/self-taught-engineer welded out of old farm machine parts. Launching would be simple enough—just pull the safety pin and the weight of all that fiberglass and metal would spin the iron-spoked winch wheel, a manure spreader wheel in its former life, and drop that big ugly boat down into the green water.

Now, would that old motor start? If it did, would it get us back to the dock or leave us stranded at the other end of the five-mile-long lake? Then, if all that went well, the boat had to be hand-cranked back out of the water, all hands grunting on that manure spreader wheel to lift the Titanic up out of the water. Most times the answer ended up being a diplomatic "No thanks, Dad. I'd rather sit here, relax, and enjoy the view."

Life moved along and after years of owning nothing bigger than a canoe, a duck boat, and an ugly fiberglass rowboat, I went looking for my own Big Boat. I was determined to learn from my dad's experience. The boat was going to be brand new, made from lightweight aluminum, and dependable. A nice 17-foot combination Fish'n'Ski caught my eye at a big boat show. I liked everything but the price. So a round of tense negotiations started with Charlie, a well-seasoned salesman who looked and talked like he'd owned a boat or two himself. These talks went nowhere until he offered up a solution. "I've got one boat left from two years ago that never sold. It's back at the shop. If you want a real deal, go have a look at that."

I did. The boat in question was a blue and grey Bluefin Fish'n'Ski—a 17-footer with a windshield, fold-down lounge seats, and a casting platform up front. Nice. But the seats were weathered from outdoor storage for two years, a used motor was mounted on the back, and it was sitting on a small trailer with skinny little wheels. I headed back to see Charlie. He really wanted to get rid of that boat. "Okay, Okay. I'll replace the seats, give you a bigger trailer, a new 50-horse motor, and throw in the Show Special—a free canvas top! Will that make you happy?"

We did the paperwork and arranged to pick the boat up in a couple of weeks. Now came a flashback to the purchase of that first old Larson with Dad. Nine year-old son Andy rode along with me to get the boat some fifty miles from home. The anticipation of a new toy was dulled when we arrived. The boat had a new trailer and motor but the seats hadn't been replaced and the canvas top wasn't installed. We went to the office and asked to talk to Charlie, expecting trouble. After getting some strange looks from the office help, the manager took us into his office and told us the bad news. "Charlie had a heart attack last week and died. What else did he say he'd give you with the boat?"

If there was any good news along with that sobering bad news, it was that the manager honored Charlie's promises and we headed home with our new boat. Rest in peace, Charlie—and thanks.

The Big Boat, as it is known, has served the family for thirty years. It's seen our sons graduate from catching sunfish to waterskiing and now to helping their own families fish and enjoy the lake. The Big Boat has taken us salmon fishing on the Great Lakes of Lake Superior and Lake Michigan. It's cruised the rocky waters at the edge of the Boundary Waters Canoe Area and pulled water skiers and tubers around the lakes near the cabin. Over those years it's also added to the stories told around the campfire. Some of these are "good news stories," like the time it was involved in a legitimate lifesaving mission.

Brother-in-law Dale and I were salmon fishing far off-shore on Lake Michigan. Probably farther off-shore than we should have been on a weekday with little other boat traffic to help us should the motor die. I was busy with the fishing gear when Dale asked, "What happened to that little sailboat we saw earlier? It disappeared and now all I see is something orange on the water."

Thanks to his awareness and sharp eyes, we quit fishing and investigated. The orange spot was the hat of one of three sailors clinging to one life jacket, with the sailboat now one hundred feet down in the forty-five degree water of Lake Michigan. They scrambled on board shivering and we headed to the Coast Guard Station at full speed. That disaster had a happy ending.

Now is boat ownership always rainbows, calm water, and sunshine? If you own a Big Boat you know the answer to that question. The Big Boat has sunk at the dock twice. Chalk those up to operator error and the need to pull the drain plug to prevent the spread of nasty invasive species. The floor has been replaced and those old lounge seats changed out to individual adjustable seats. Along the way there have been dents, dock rash, failed batteries, and a bent axle on the trailer. In Big Boat terms, that's small stuff—even if Cabela's did send me their hardcover catalogue as a gift the year after I replaced the floor, seats, and a few other items. Let's talk about the original motor.

The motor Charlie threw in with the deal was a

brand that is now known to all boaters to be less than reliable. It is no longer manufactured. The brand name starts with an "F." It contains more than four letters, but to me it has become the "F Word" of boat motors. It cannot be uttered in my presence without adding a quarter to the Swear Jar. The Swear Jar would be full many times over if I had been forced to throw in a quarter every time I used the real "F Word" when wrestling with that motor.

It was a great motor for the first five years. Then things started happening, expensive things. I won't relate them all. That would require a book, not a chapter. I'll just relate the incident that resulted in its replacement with a more expensive, reliable Mercury motor. Marcie and I loaded the dogs in the boat and headed out on Crooked Lake for a relaxing evening cruise. We made it halfway across the lake when the motor smoked, stuttered, and died. Based on past experience with the same symptoms, multiple times, I knew that I'd soon be handing the local outboard mechanic a five-hundred-dollar check or my credit card. Marcie knew that, too.

She said the real "F Word," or words like it, a few times along with me. Then she bluntly stated—"I am not stepping into this boat again until you get a new motor—and not an 'F Word,' 'F Word' motor!"

Yes, it was that bad—my wife actually ordered me to spend money on a boat.

I know I'm not alone when it comes to having Big Boat problems. My next youngest brother should be smarter; he is a real rocket scientist after all. But the family obsession with boats did not skip him. He keeps a forty-something-year-old sailboat docked up on

Lake Superior and has a few stories of his own. I was along as a witness to one. We were cruising the water of Gitche Gumee under the power of the boat's little forty-something diesel engine when Steve noticed the bilge pump running constantly, spraying water out the side. "Why is that running?" he asked. A quick look below provided the answer. The engine was still running despite a hole blown out its side, with the cold, clear water of Lake Superior flooding the boat via that hole. In case you're wondering, that engine replacement had a price tag that included five numbers before any decimal points.

I know other boat owners are now running through their minds the many sayings relating to boat ownership—sayings that are mighty funny to anyone who does not own a Big Boat. Things like: "The bigger the boat, the bigger the Boob." "A boat is a hole in the water you pour money into." "The two happiest days of my life were the day I bought the boat, and the day I sold the boat." "A boat owner and his money are soon parted."

Personally, I think the most accurate is a combination of these and is advice well considered —"The bigger the boat, the bigger the bills!"

The Perfect Deer Stand

It's time for a walk with three hours of daylight left on a perfect December afternoon. A walk to visit a favorite spot, the perfect deer stand. Last night's snow dusted the forest and the thin ice of the lake. The thermometer on the cabin's deck hasn't reached thirty and won't. But the perfect deer stand will be warm and comfortable on one of the last days of deer season, one of the last days before winter.

The deer stand is on the other side of the lake, across half a mile of water in the warm months. Water is not a factor now with the lake covered with four inches of smooth, clear ice and ringed with white snow frosting. It provides a smooth inviting highway, safe enough to leapfrog from island to island, hugging shores, tip-toeing across channels. The channels funnel the wind, turning a light northwesterly breeze into a mild wind chill, burning the eyes and nipping the nose before reaching the next sheltering shore. There's no need to sneak at this point. The far island and the steep bank of the main shore will keep alarming sights, sounds, and smells from the wary senses of the forest deer. I'm alone. The only other signs of life are the straight tracks of a fox moving north to south.

The steep hillside at the edge of the forest requires a decision. Circle to the right, find an easy incline but longer path up through the dogwood and hazelnut brush? Or sneak straight up the hill and directly to the stand, arriving out of breath, without tainting the woods? I chose the short, hard way, up the hill, reaching ahead for trees to leverage, ducking under one branch while another claws at my clothes, back pack, and gun. Yes, there's a gun. It is deer season after all.

Just ahead, the perfect deer stand waits on top of the ridge. A giant pine once stood on the crest. It now lies rotting on the forest floor. Needles gone, branches broken, a mere skeleton of its once mighty self. Just short of the upturned root ball is the perfect place to sit. The two-foot trunk provides a wide seat made softer and drier by a foam cushion from the backpack. The twisted upturned roots secure the Thermos of coffee while blocking the cold breeze and providing a comfy back support.

To the right, through the screening of a mix of red and white pines, is the wide expanse of an upland swamp. In the summer, beavers slap tails on the open water in the daylight and build their log mansion high by night. The osprey wings lazy circles overhead, on guard, chirping to her chicks while waiting for her mate to return with fish. Ducks cut ripples across calm water. Today it's a desolate frosted wasteland. The beaver house is a white mound in the snow-covered ice. The osprey nest an empty pile of sticks atop a long dead pine. The ducks, gone to warmer climates.

Straight ahead is shelter. A deep valley running from swamp to lake, park-like and open on the bottom with mature pines and oaks, overgrown with brush and spindly aspen up the sides and top. The perfect place for deer to stroll on a December afternoon.

To the left is the south bay of the lake, barely visible through the bare limbs of aspen and birch, further screened by rust-brown leaves clinging to oaks. Hidden, but on this chilly day easily heard. The thin young ice still maturing, growing pains ringing through the forest like wedding spoons against good glass, high pitched now, soon to be lower as ice builds and winter throws down a thick blanket of snow.

The sun moves on while a cup of coffee warms hands and insides, while eyes search for movement. The flick of an ear. The disruption of a shadow or sunbeam. A whole deer dropped into the scene by nature's magic.

Every perfect deer stand has more than just a view. At the edge of the osprey swamp, a clump of grass nods a dark bent top in the breeze, making the heart skip a beat until the brain recognizes it for what it is. A flap of white birch bark peeling from its parent tree flaps in the wind, drawing attention each time a mild breeze eases through the pines. A red squirrel scurries about, up tree, down tree, digging in the pine needle carpet, chattering each time it looks uphill at the orange-dressed intruder. The chickadees and nuthatches engage in cheerful chatter, digging in bark cracks and crevices, cocking heads to examine each in close detail, flying down to perch on the gun barrel pointed downhill.

Yes, this is the perfect deer stand. The setting sun beaming in through pines, warming the body and heart while the lake sings, the grass clump bobs and nods, the bark flaps, and the squirrel and the chickadees carry on. No, there aren't any deer. That doesn't really matter. Today this place is perfect without them.

Jim's First and Last Deer Hunt
by Jim Lein

Note: This next story was written by my younger brother, Jim. He's a writer, musician, father, ski patrol member, and a few other things out west in Colorado. One thing he is not, is a hunter. That's okay. I make no apologies for being a lifelong hunter but don't expect that everyone, even a brother, will share my passion. Here's his perspective.

Deer hunting is the common bond across all hunters. Every boy gazing down the road to manhood wants to kill a deer and eat it. Growing up in rural Minnesota, learning to handle a gun was a ubiquitous rite of passage. I dabbled in all sorts of hunting— beast and bird—with my dad and older brother, Mike. But my heart wasn't in it because I believed then as I do now that you shouldn't kill an animal unless you are going to eat it or it plans to eat you.

But I loved Mom's venison stew and optimistically embarked on my first deer hunt soon after I took my firearms safety certification classes —"gun training"—as we called it. We drove forty miles north to the Watson Sag, where the endless and homogeneous farmland droops for a few miles in a glacial channel of verdant grassland, cottonwood groves, and shallow sloughs. Our party of about ten friends and relatives hunted the better part of the day but came up empty-handed.

"Let's see if we can flush something out of that cornfield and get Jimmy his first deer," announced Dad.

The rest of the party fanned out at one end while Mike and I walked a couple hundred yards along the perimeter of a sea of head-high, golden stalks heavy with ripe ears. Everything I owned was hand-me-down, from my jacket to my underwear to the single-shot 20-gauge shotgun I carried. My brother brandished his beloved 12-gauge pump.

"Put a bird load in," Mike advised. "They're more likely to scare up a pheasant. Keep the slug in your vest pocket where it's easy to get at."

I obliged and we took up positions at opposite ends of a gap where a rutted farm road split the field. My dad signaled and the party entered the cornrows at the other end. We could hear them ominously crashing through the field, hoping to spook a deer across the gap we now defended. I suddenly had to pee and I turned to the side to relieve myself, cradling the shotgun in the crook of my arm.

Midstream, I glanced over my shoulder to see a young buck stick its head out of the stalks. My heart leapt. Still peeing, I opened the barrel of the 20-gauge. The unused shell ejected past my ear with a whoosh. I reached in my vest for the slug only to discover a shell-sized hole in the bottom of the pocket. The deer tiptoed across the gap. My brother, initially confused by my hunting tactic of turning *away* from the prey, motioned wildly for me to stand clear but by the time I zipped up, the only thing visible was a fleeting glimpse of a white tail.

I took a lot of ribbing for the rest of the day, to the verge of tears. The three of us bid good hunting to the rest of the party and loaded up the station wagon to drive north to happier hunting grounds in the deep forests of the Iron Range. After a cold, sleepless night in a canvas tent, we set out on the trail early into the towering trees. The air was brittle and smelled of pine. The fallen oak leaves crunched under our boots. After about an hour we came to an intersection of trails.

"Jimmy, you stand behind those fallen trees," my dad said. "Mike and I will head down these trails and see if we can flush anything your way."

I vowed to remain vigilant. The forest swallowed them up, leaving me alone and scared in a mysterious, dark woodland. The leaves rustled behind me and I spun around, shotgun leveled. Nothing. I scanned the forest and heard the rustling again. Right at my feet! I looked down and saw a cute little field mouse scurry under a log. I squatted down on my haunches and carefully lifted a branch. The mouse looked up at me quizzically.

I propped my shotgun against a tree, sat down, and leaned back against the fallen logs. Soon, I had a dozen mice scrambling around my legs and torso. It was kind of a *Gulliver's Travels* moment but I was pinned down not by midgets with ropes but rather by rodents with charm. Some immeasurable time passed until I heard my father call out from down the trail. I jumped up, mice flying everywhere, grabbed my shotgun, and assumed what I perceived to be a hunter's stance.

"See anything?" Mike asked as they walked up.

"Nothin'," I answered, shaking my head disgustedly. Truth be told, a herd of moose could have thundered through the intersection and I would have been oblivious.

We struck out across the forest and, half an hour later, Mike spooked a doe from behind a fallen tree and dropped her with one shot. I excitedly fired my gun in the air above his head. He spun around with a deer-in-the-headlights look and probably would have knocked me to the ground if he hadn't been so excited himself.

The afternoon shadows were getting long as I watched my dad and brother field-dress the deer and cut it in half to carry out. Since I was a scrawny hundred pounds, they slung the front half on a pole and headed down the trail, leaving me guarding the business end of the carcass.

"I'll shoot anything that moves!" I, the scaredy cat, called after them. "I swear!"

My brother looked back over his shoulder with a "man up" stare.

I survived a lonely couple of hours without incident though even the mice had abandoned me. My dad and brother hailed me from afar to avoid any accidental fraternal bloodshed. Back home, friends and family considered the hunt a big success and I—by association—part of that success, like getting an assist on a big goal in a hockey game. As far as I know, Dad and my brother never spoke a word of my timidity. I didn't tell either of them about the mice. I never hunted again and, consequently, the world is a safer place.

The Chili Incident

The Chili Incident

Sometimes my deep-rooted sense of Scandinavian decency compels me to warn readers that the contents of a story might be offensive, crude, or not politically correct, depending on their own deep-rooted senses. This is one of those stories. One that has been embellished many times at our long-time deer hunting camp. A story that fellow members of the group have implored me to write so that it may be professionally and factually immortalized before it is further embellished and thus becomes a fable, not a factual account of the actual incident.

To start with, you need to understand the inner workings of our deer camp culture. Five of us so-called adults started it over thirty-five years ago when one of the guys' family farms was vacated. Thus the house and property became available for hunting. Over the years the membership has changed somewhat due to various personal and private situations. However, currently three of us charter members remain to enjoy the comradery of the camp and the hunt together with our semi-adult offspring. Or I should say "usually" enjoy the hunt. Sometimes tensions arise and the resulting remedy to easing the tensions result in things such as "The Chili Incident."

For example, I love to cook and I think I'm pretty good at it. Cooking was one way I found to attract girls back in those bachelor college days. You might say I was driven by primal urges to become a good cook. A little home-cooked spaghetti, a loaf of garlic bread, a jug of wine—you could always hope something good was going to become of it. But I digress. Steve, another charter deer camp member, also loves to cook and is damn good at it. He does wild game and old home-style Scandinavian recipes as good as any TV chef. Need an example? I will even eat lutefisk if HE fixes it. Enough said.

Steve also happens to be a messy cook. This spells trouble in the cozy confines of the deer camp kitchen. His turkey noodle soup, utilizing the scraps from the traditional Friday night turkey dinner along with made-from-scratch egg noodles, is a go-to hot lunch after a long morning in a cold deer stand. However, the kitchen looks like a flour-filled bomb went off after he is done throwing the items together. So I have relinquished any role in cooking. I stay out of his way and move in quickly after the pots are on the stove. I have become the camp's Chief Dish Washer and Kitchen Cleaner.

That brings us to The Chili Incident. Around five years ago most of us showed up at deer camp, a.k.a. The Farm, on the Friday before opening day. Steve had arrived the night before and had got down to cooking. This year the special Friday night meal was chili. Bubbling away on the stove was a vast pot of it containing fresh tomatoes, onions, two kinds of peppers from Steve's ample home garden, and four-year-old venison found in the bottom of his freezer during cleanout. Note that the kitchen looked like a chili fixin's bomb had gone off so I had work to do. The chili itself looked like something a southwestern witch might have brewed up but a cautious taste proved that Steve hadn't lost his touch.

We dug in. Many bowls of chili were consumed around the famed and storied kitchen table, as neighbors dropped in to visit and while stories of past camp adventures were told and retold, becoming more epic as the night wore on and more adult beverages were served up alongside the next bowl of chili. All seemed well as members checked out to their sleeping quarters, each to their own schedule and level of desire to see the sun rise from a deer stand.

I heard no complaints early the next morning as hunters awoke to their own schedules, consumed breakfast to their liking of anything from a granola bar and cup of coffee to Steve and his son Robbie's usual huge bacon, onions, peppers, potatoes, and eggs scramble. I stayed in to clean up. Most opening days I let the more driven hunters have the good stands while I clean the disaster the kitchen has become after a night's partying and the breakfast rush. With that accomplished and the sun well up, I parked myself in the front yard in a comfortable chair with a cup of coffee and a pair of binoculars. I was a spectator, watching the deer stands from the stands.

I noticed two things pretty quickly. One, I did not hear the usual scattering of rifle shots from the six stands out in the woods to the west. It appeared that the opening day deer were not showing up. Two, I did notice that the members in the three elevated tree stands I could observe were not spending much time up in the stand. An orange-clad hunter would appear in a stand, sit motionless for ten or fifteen minutes, and then climb down out of sight for an extended period of time. I considered several possibilities—leaving the stand to check sign, checking on a newer hunter, helping field-dress or track a deer shot before I took my seat, things like that. As it turned out, none of these where the case.

By late morning exhausted, feeble-looking hunters started to straggle back to the house. Four of the six had the same story. Shortly after arriving at their stands under the cover of predawn darkness, disaster struck. Or should I say the chili struck and disaster and/or the chili kept on striking, forcing the afflicted to scramble down the steps of their deer stands for the dreaded task of answering nature's call far from the comfortable heated confines of the house bathroom.

Now here come some of the graphic details. I'll warn you again. Feel free to skip the next paragraphs if you are easily offended or have a weak stomach.

While two members reported no symptoms, the other four hunting on the farm reported multiple trips each up and down the ladders of their deer stands. At least one admitted that a trip resulted in "an accident" halfway down the ladder. He further admitted that a pair of black briefs had been sacrificed to the depths of the swamp next to his stand. A complaint common to all was that not enough toilet paper had been packed. In fact, they all were sure that enough toilet paper could not have been packed for what had just transpired. The discussion soon turned to graphic details as they tried to one-up each other with how they had dealt with their individual cases. Those details need not be further recounted here.

My oldest son showed up late after hunting a neighboring property. He reported similar symptoms and had his own story regarding the sleeve of a long sleeved T-shirt that had been sliced off with a hunting knife to make up for the lack of enough toilet paper. It's worth noting that no deer had been seen or shot by any members. It might have been lack of deer, which sometimes happens. It could have been that these hunters were having a hard time focusing on seeing deer. Or it could be the fact that deer have a very acute sense of smell.

Now, in fairness to Steve's cooking, I must add a few details to this story. Note that I am a trained Environmental Health professional who is often forced to listen to the sordid details of data collected from outbreaks of food-borne illness at public establishments. Thus I have a strong stomach for these types of things and some professional interest. This case of the chili trots intrigued me to do postmortem interviews with the afflicted and the non-afflicted to get to the bottom of the cause.

First of all, the afflicted had two things in common. One, they had happily consumed vast quantities of the homemade chili twelve to fifteen hours before the symptoms manifested themselves. Along with the chili, they had also happily consumed various adult beverages including celebratory shots of a camp favorite—a fine German liquor with a picture of deer on the label, best served straight-up straight from the freezer.

Now here lies the telltale facts that help solve

cases like this. Darrell and his twelve-year-old son Carson reported no symptoms. This in spite of the fact that Carson had deemed this chili "the best ever" and had consumed amounts only possible by a twelve-year-old growing boy appetite. In fact, he dug into another bowl while the interviews were taking place. This was against the recommendation of his father and had a secondary effect of sending several of the afflicted group scrambling to be the first through the narrow door of the bathroom. His father had refrained from chili consumption altogether. I'm not saying Darrell didn't trust Steve's cooking. I think he's just not a big fan of chili. Also note that Carson had not indulged in any adult beverages for obvious reasons.

So that narrowed it down. Delicious home-made chili plus the fine German hunting elixir equaled bad things. Over and over again.

Now there was one mystery. I had sat in my favorite chair at the kitchen table the night before, back to wall, enjoying the comradery of my partners and the friendly neighbors who stopped by, consuming both chili and that magic German elixir. And I was just fine, not suffering any symptoms other than those that could be commonly expected from such a night. Why not me too? What powerful antidote did my digestive system hold? I mocked my weak fellow hunters and cast shame upon their abilities. I did refrain from eating any more of the chili.

You might be guessing where this is going. The next morning I became a member of the afflicted group. While I had the warm bathroom and ample toilet paper close by as I again refrained from hunting, I soon learned what others had gone through. As they returned for lunch throughout the day, I suffered from both the affliction and their much-deserved mocking of my brave words from the day before.

So there you have it. The Chili Incident. A true story. One that needs no further embellishment or details but deserves to be immortalized for the history of the world. Or at least our deer camp.

I do apologize again to my faithful readers who might have bypassed my warning at the beginning of the story, and the middle of the story, and are now offended or disgusted. So feel free to ask for a refund. Or you could just rip these pages out of the book and use them for toilet paper, out in the deer stand, if you didn't bring "enough."

Minnesota Nice

I checked myself in the truck's rear view mirror, combed the fuzzies out of my beard, and had one last look around camp. It was almost time to make a move. This was going to be a bit more difficult than the last two nights but I was confident. After all, this wasn't my first time.

My next victims were parked in the shade of an aspen grove about one hundred yards to the east. It was just them and me, camped way out here at the trailhead in the remote Montana backcountry with no one else around for miles. They had driven past me on the way into their camp and had a good look at me and the bloody meat bags hanging in the trees. Hopefully what they saw was a successful gray-haired hunter camping out in a battered old pickup truck. Harmless and lonely, without even a warming campfire in the chill of a late autumn Montana evening.

I had a plan. My neighbors had pulled up to their camp in one sweet-looking truck—a late model extended-cab four-wheel drive with a cool-looking gear rack bolted to the top of a custom-painted topper. Best of all, it had Montana license plates. That was a good thing, good for me at least.

Back in my home state we have a saying that, roughly translated, means Minnesotans tend to be trustworthy, polite, passive, and friendly—even with total strangers. We are "Minnesota Nice." Personally, I've found Montanans to be every bit as friendly, and

unfortunately for them, more gullible. "Montana Nice,"
if you will. These guys looked no different than the
others I had crossed paths with.

I had a plan. My neighbors' camp consisted of a
cushy-looking motor home and a smaller trailer. From
the looks of these and their truck, they must have
some really good stuff. I'd wander over and act the
part of a typical trustworthy, polite, passive,
friendly Minnesotan. Experience told me they would be
willing to talk about the truck and their luxurious
camp. They'd let their guard down and never realize
what I was really up to. After all, I was "Minnesota
Nice."

I considered accessories, pulled on a worn camo
baseball cap with a seed corn company logo, and opened
a can of beer while waiting for the sun to set just a
bit more. I didn't want them to get too close a look
at me. A week of living out of the back of my truck
far off the beaten path hadn't done much for my
appearance, even if you ignored the blood stains.

The previous two nights hadn't been much of a
challenge. Two young adult males, old enough to drink
and old enough to be out on their own, camping by
themselves in the boonies, forty miles from nowhere.
They had been cocky and confident, but then that was
mainly the cheap beer talking. All I had to do was
wander over to their campfire, talk about hunting and
fishing for a while, and, well, the rest just kinda
got out of hand.

I did learn a lot from those youngsters while I
suckered them in. Like the fact that Montana is run,
for better or worse, by ranchers and lawyers—at least

in their opinion. And that a certain Detroit truck-maker with a horned sheep head for a logo makes the best @#$%^& diesel engine currently available in the USA. That "USA" qualifier was added due to their professed knowledge of a conspiracy by domestic truck companies to prevent a certain Japanese manufacturer from importing diesel engines.

I also learned that out-of-state hunters from the east and west coasts should be wary out here in the middle of nowhere. Those two young bucks might get cocky and make a little trouble for the interlopers. But I was okay. I was from Minnesota. I was "Minnesota Nice."

Like I said, those young men never realized what happened. I nodded my head at their smart talk and asked a few dumb questions, taking my time and stretching the fun out for two nights. By that second night, they were distracted, rooting around in their supplies, looking for more food and beer, and blaming each other for what was missing. That was the last I saw of them—honest.

But as they say, that was then, this was now. I made a final adjustment to the hat and started down the dirt road to my current neighbors, thinking about a few of my other targets. Like the guys from Kalispell a few years ago on my first trip west. They all felt sorry for me, camping out in a truck, sleeping in the back alongside the carcass of a recently deceased whitetail. They ran a dry camp—no alcohol allowed. But they compensated for the lack of booze.

One of their sons was a gourmet Tex/Mex chef and didn't mind putting his skills to good use in elk camp. It's a little known fact that good food tends to loosen tongues and lessen inhibitions just as fast as bad booze. I played along, ate their food, and lulled them into a false sense of security while pretending to enjoy their old stories. They never had a clue. Hell, they even inducted me into their exclusive one-shot one-kill club, gave me their addresses, and invited me back next year. I made a clean getaway early the next morning, just before a sloppy, late-October snow storm closed all the backcountry roads.

Of course it isn't always simple. There was that one group. Three generations of elk hunters sitting around the same fire. Things looked easy enough—especially after I turned down a shot of top shelf booze in favor of the cheap crap the half-a-dozen young male cousins were swilling. But those boys got a bit cranky after their dads and grandpa went to sleep. Even threatened to throw my truck tires on the fire when I dissed their smoky pine firewood and bitched about high nonresident license fees.

I learned a couple of lessons there. Never complain to a resident hunter about the injustice of spendy nonresident license fees and, like the old saying goes, never knock another man's dog—or campfire, in this case. I cut my losses and left early, slipping away into the night and back to my camp. They had the numbers and the testosterone for once. There would be others. Like these guys tonight.

I ambled over, making sure they saw me approaching in the dim light. I took it slow, enjoying my beer, and acting the part of a successful tired hunter. A mid-thirties male gave me a smile as his elderly father walked over. They each had an after-the-hunt drink sitting comfortably in their hands. I gave them a tried-and-true opening line. "Hi there! Say, couldn't help but notice that good-looking truck. Love the color. What year is it? I'm thinking about trading off my old beast."

The young guy beamed as he swirled the ice in his drink and launched into a detailed description of his pet truck. His dad, a trim-looking guy in his early seventies, joined in. "You from Minnesota? I've got a good friend back there who builds muzzleloader guns. Good people there!"

That was all it took. It was "Minnesota Nice" meets "Montana Nice," just as planned. I spent a half hour with them, talking trucks, guns, and hunting. Then they threw me a twist. Their wives exited the motor home and introduced themselves before starting to cook up what looked to be a real tasty meal. I hadn't planned on women being around. As darkness cloaked the valley, I thanked them for the truck info, wished them well, and politely retired to regroup. They didn't offer to replenish my beer. But I had a feeling about this—and a new plan. This could be my best score ever. All it would take was some patience and a little extra effort.

I fired up my one-burner lantern, strategically hung it by the back of the truck, and sat on the tailgate at the edge of its dim glow. I imagined what the scene looked like from the other camp—a lonely guy from Minnesota, in the dark night, a long way from home and family, tired, harmless, and hungry.

It worked—I'm getting good at this. About a half hour later the beam of a flashlight broke free from the camp and headed my way. I expected the son or his dad. But I had really fooled them. The young guy's wife walked up to my truck, totally unsuspecting and carrying a plate of food that an old lone wolf like me couldn't even dream up.

Grilled marinated lamb chops from a prize 4-H lamb, topped with a little mint jelly, served alongside an ample portion of grilled asparagus, and baby red potatoes sautéed in olive oil and rosemary. I gave her my best smile and honest assurances that lamb was one of my favorites. I sweet-talked her for a minute or two and politely waited until she turned to walk back before I pulled my razor-sharp, custom-made Finnish knife from its hidden sheath.

As it turned out, I didn't really need it. That damn lamb was so tender I could cut it with my plastic fork!

Lost and Found

Someday, perhaps many years in the future, an archaeologist might be wandering around northern Minnesota or central Montana and find a trail of old relics. Spread across this landscape, in what are hopefully still beautiful wild and remote places, he, she, or it, might find a rusted faded fishing lure buried in the bank of a river. A pair of sunglasses crushed under the gravel of an ancient road. A billfold full of curious plastic cards and a few crumbling bits of colored paper. A series of knives with rusted blades. Flashlights with long dead batteries and shattered lenses. Perhaps the technology of the time will be able to trace them to their owner. But in case that technology doesn't get developed, I write this in explanation. It was me.

This problem started over forty years ago and is getting worse with age. It first surfaced back in those years spent at a northern Minnesota college known for outdoor sports opportunities. A group of us trekked off into the national forest and spent a day hunting grouse deep in the woods. I was successful at one point and pulled out a small sheath knife to field-dress the bird alongside a scenic brook. The knife was a small "Western" brand with a high carbon steel three-inch blade and pretty rosewood handle. It cost more than a poor college student should have spent. With the dirty work done, the knife was rinsed and placed on a handy rock while the bird and my hands

were washed. The hunt continued. To the best of my
knowledge, the knife remains there to this day, deep
in the woods at a spot that can't be found again.

Knives seemed to be the thing to lose in those
early years. They were used for a task, set down, and
forgotten or overlooked while dealing with other
issues. Then optical equipment, things like pre-
scription sunglasses and binoculars, took over. This
may be why I have ignored trends and advertisements
for spendy high-quality gear and buy this stuff at
discount stores. On one hunting expedition, a side
trip had to be made to buy a new pair of cheap
binoculars since the ones packed for the trip were
lost before arriving at the destination. At least I
hadn't lost the emergency credit card—yet.

A more typical scenario unfolded several years
ago in the wilds of Montana. I hiked out onto a high
country plateau and spent the sunny afternoon
surveying coulees through a spotting scope, looking
for the right mule deer buck. I didn't find the right
one, walked back to the truck under the setting sun
and headed east to Minnesota for a rendezvous at deer
camp. My sunglasses seemed to get buried in the messy
truck and weren't to be found. Their location became
more of a mystery after decluttering the truck at
home. Months later I searched the equipment inventory
in vain for the spotting scope.

I jumped to conclusions and assumed they had
been left a mile out in the Montana uplands, next to
the dead tree used to steady the spotting scope. The
location was remote but there was a chance it could be
found. Two years later I did just that, walking back

across the mile of broken ground and finding the tree.
The sunglasses and spotting scope weren't there. Found
and claimed by another hunter or cowboy? I have found
a few things myself and enjoyed the thrill of
discovery without much thought to the loser's loss.
Dropped from an open zipper on the backpack on the
hike out? A nice knife had met that fate a few years
before only miles from the same location. Left on the
truck bumper in the fading light? We have all probably
found someone else's roadkill equipment.

Oldest son, Andy, was waiting back at the truck
and had the answer. He went with the roadkill option.
"Face it," he said. "You left them on the truck bumper
and someone else now is squinting through cheap
sunglasses and swearing at the blurry view in that
crappy spotting scope."

I said nothing. Until we got in the truck and
starting driving away. At this point his expensive
binoculars slid off the roof of the truck, down onto
the windshield, and ended up dangling from a
windshield wiper right in front of his face. I managed
to get a picture of the scene despite being overcome
by laughter. This could be a hereditary defect.

My smugness over that incident lasted about two
weeks. I was sitting at the deer camp kitchen table
when he walked up from the basement and handed over
the long-gone sunglasses and spotting scope. They had
spent the last two years on a chair in the basement,
covered by a blanket. I guess that shows how often the
deer camp gets cleaned.

Now the age of electronics has arrived and, with
it, the age of lost electronics. While packing for

another adventure, extra time was spent making sure that batteries were charged and user instructions were reviewed. All the gadgets were checked off as they were placed in one handy plastic bag. Waterproof camera—check. Mini-video camera—check. GPS—check. Emergency satellite locator—check. Headlamp and solar rechargeable flashlight—check and check. The bag was then dropped into the backpack all ready for action. Or so I thought.

Upon arriving back in the badlands of Montana, they were not to be found. Not one of them. After a day or two of agonizing and bitching about the loss, I decided they were probably lying on the garage floor back home or tucked into some secret compartment of the new truck. I carried on without electronic guidance or emergency alert capabilities, using a smart phone to document the trip and hoping no legs got broke miles from a road and phone coverage. The return home did not solve the mystery. There was no bag on the garage floor or in a secret truck compartment or the basement storage area or anywhere else.

This incident caused worry-filled, sleepless nights. This was not just one semi-expensive knife. Not a pair of inexpensive sunglasses and a cheap spotting scope. Or a five-dollar flashlight. This was over a thousand dollars' worth of equipment. On about the third day of agonizing and retracing steps, there came a revelation. I'm not sure what caused me to think of this possibility. I followed some sub-conscious hunch, went downstairs, and opened up the chest freezer. Yes, there, snuggled right next to the plastic bag of frozen meat that had been packed and forgotten for the Montana trip, was another plastic bag of solidly frozen electronic equipment.

I followed expert advice and wrapped them in a thick sleeping bag to slowly defrost. They all appear to have survived ten days in the freezer. While these electronic gizmos may be fine, I believe I have now lost my reputation with friends and family, my ego, and a good part of my sanity. The only hope for the return of these may lie with that future archaeologist mentioned earlier. Maybe he or she will have time travel ability by then and return these to me if and when they are found.

Creative Financing
for Hunters—
Or How to Beat the
High Cost of Hunting

This story is meant to be read only by hunters, whether they be male or female. It is not meant to be read by non-hunting partners of said group. The author will not be held responsible for any harm to relationships and/or monetary revenge that comes from violation of this warning.

Let's face it, fellow hunters. Pursuing wild game, be it four-footed or feathered, can be an expensive proposition, even if you're fortunate enough to live in an area that's overrun with critters and fowl. It's much worse for those who choose to pursue game away from local stomping grounds and must therefore try to justify gas, motel rooms, and other related travel costs, not to mention non-resident license fees to Significant Others. I've become very creative in financing hunting excursions and would like to offer some free advice.

First of all, make sure the Significant Other enjoys the rewards of your hunts. Brush up on your cooking and wine selection skills. We all know that properly cared for and prepared wild game is some of the best-tasting meat on the planet, and it's good for both of you. Learn a few good recipes and do the cooking once in a while. I'd suggest something a bit more unique and romantic than charring an elk rib eye on the grill or throwing a pheasant into a crock pot of mushroom soup. Make sure to mention how expensive free-range, pasture-raised organic meat is at the upscale market downtown. You are not being cheap! Pair the entree with a good bottle of wine and make it a special occasion.

A word of caution here. Given that a skilled hunter like you can provide the main course for many "special" meals, exercise some care and a little frugality when selecting the wine. Even a ten-dollar bottle is going to add up and cut into the hunting fund. You do the math.

Don't despair if your cooking skills are lacking or if you're down on your hunting luck. There's plenty more you can do. Start by making sure your partner knows how frugal you are. A picture of an attractive young bartender serving you a martini in a hunting lodge's hot tub is not going to score any points at home. Fortunately, I'm a do-it-yourselfer and don't have that problem. When I hit the road, I stay in hotels that are so cheap I am embarrassed to say what they cost. I don't take pictures of them for fear my wife might worry about me bringing home some nasty surprise. I do share pictures of my bunk in the back of the truck or the snow on the roof of the tent, just to prove I was roughing it and not enjoying myself.

I also literally save my pennies to help pay expenses and I make sure she knows it. A fruit jar with a hole in the lid sits prominently on the bedroom dresser. Every night I make a ritual of emptying my pocket change into it while remarking on how much gas money is being saved for the next trip.

Now we come to the tricky part. I suppose you could call it "creative financing," or "fuzzy economics," but those seem like such negative and deceptive terms. Think of it this way: how would respected people like long-term politicians or Wall Street high-rollers justify financing a hunting trip to a constituent or client?

Let's start with those high non-resident license fees. Montana gets over a thousand dollars for a non-resident deer/elk combination license. (I really hope my wife heeds the warning and doesn't read this!) You can apply for an elk-only license for about a hundred dollars less but the combo license is a much better value. Value is what we are after.

That's a lot of money unless you look at it from a different perspective. The combination license includes a deer license. A deer-only license is about six hundred bucks. So subtract that and the elk license only really costs four hundred. You have already made elk hunting cheaper than deer hunting. Who can argue with that? But wait, there's more! This license also includes a year's worth of fishing, a seventy-dollar value, and a small game license, a hundred-dollar value. Subtract these and that elk tag in a prime western state is only really setting you back a little more than a hundred dollars.

Now there's the trip expense—gas, food, spirits, and the like. I know from past experience that an elk hunting trip to Montana will put about 2,200 miles on the truck's odometer. Those miles will cause my pickup to drink about 115 gallons of gas or around three-hundred-fifty-dollars' worth at three bucks a gallon—maybe more if those politicians and Wall Street types have screwed around with the oil market lately. That cost can easily be cut in half if another paying hunter rides along. On the other hand, non-paying freeloaders like the first-born son will add weight, drag down gas mileage, and increase other expenses such as food and beer. You have to weigh the pros and cons and decide for yourself what's best. However, there is another way to cut this expense.

Get real. It's fall. It's hunting season somewhere for something. You are not just going to stay home and rake leaves! In my case, I would likely spend a couple weekends at my cabin doing stuff like duck hunting, grouse hunting, and working on deer stands. Two trips to the cabin can easily eat up over a thousand miles or about half of an elk hunting trip's mileage. Therefore any reasonable politician or financial guru would surely advise us to deduct these miles from the out-of-state trip, thus drastically reducing travel costs. Note that this would-have-done-something-anyway philosophy works even better for food and booze. You eat and drink at home, don't you? Bingo! Subtract a week's worth of groceries and beer from trip expenses!

Next is some very simple advice with no dollar signs needed. I seriously recommend that you do not impulse-buy highly visible, expensive equipment in the name of hunting—things like ATVs, guns, and pickups. Many Significant Others view shopping as a recreational sport and love the thrill of the hunt. However, most are smart enough to recognize a four-or-five-figure purchase for what it is—a mortgage payment or maybe an all-inclusive trip for two to a warm climate in the dead of winter.

You have to be creative. Add some romance and

maybe a few big vague words when dealing with large purchases. You need that two-seater ATV so that you can ride together and strengthen your relationship while mutually bonding with nature. And that custom-built rifle in 350 Whiz Bang Magnum is really only pennies a day when "amortized" over a lifetime. Just keep in mind that some purchases carry more risks than others. That custom gun purchase can backfire real quickly if your Significant Other, like mine, knows a thing or two about guns and likes to use them. They may want their own, which will then double that outlay.

I may not be a rocket scientist, but I think this is all logical and adds up. The bottom line is that hunting trips don't have to be expensive. In fact, it may be possible to claim you're actually making money chasing wild critters, depending on how creative you are and how reasonable that Significant Other is.

One final word of advice. I strongly suggest that you don't convert this scheme into an easy-to-understand spreadsheet to further prove how frugal you are. I am pretty sure that will never pay off.

Winter Grouse

If you have ever been exposed to colonial American history or sporting art, you may have seen old oil-on-canvas paintings of an idyllic autumn hunting scene. The setting is a woodsy New England trail, lined with fall colors. A grouse is flushing ahead of a leather-clad frontiersman who swings a flintlock shotgun while his dog, some kind of brown and white setter, watches, waiting for the retrieve. Well, that's not the picture I'm about to paint.

This grouse hunt starts in the December Minnesota forest, a place devoid of most colors except white snow, gray skies, brown leafless trees, and dull green pines. Add half a foot of snow to below freezing temperatures and we have left that idyllic New England landscape behind.

I had been sneaking around the forest with a muzzleloading deer rifle, taking part in the late muzzleloader deer season. The deer left over from the regular hunting season were showing nothing but tracks. What I had seen were ruffed grouse, taunting me from trees, flushing across open swamps, and clucking from atop stumps. I resisted those temptations for four days. Then on a snowy afternoon, I left the rifle behind and loaded the SUV with a muzzleloading double-barrel shotgun and Sage, the nine-month-old Labrador puppy. That's when the trouble started. My upgraded, tricked-out off-road SUV lost all four-wheel drive capabilities. Heading up the unplowed road into the miles of state forest surrounding the cabin turned into a white knuckle ride, a give-er'-hell-and-hope affair.

The first spot featured a small lake with spruce-lined shores and a hilltop parking spot where I had a chance of getting the lame SUV moving again. Half of the lake's perimeter had been logged years ago and was a thick mess of aspen regrowth and thorny raspberry canes—just the stuff winter grouse love. I followed Sage out onto the ice, crunching along the perimeter while she crashed through the undergrowth, hunting rabbits, squirrels, mice, tweety birds, and maybe grouse.

It was easy to pretend we were old-time trappers searching the nooks and crannies of the shore for signs of fur bearers. Mink, otter, and fishers had left their marks in the fresh snow. A big beaver lodge was complete with food cache marked by aspen and willow branches poking up through the ice. Even a few deer and turkeys had cut across narrow points, using the lake ice for a handy highway like wildlife and humans had for thousands of years.

The grouse seemed to be lying low, maybe due to the lack of sunshine and random snowflakes drifting down through twenty-five-degree air. The dog and I wandered for two hours before heading back to our starting point via an overgrown logging trail. Crossing the trail in the raspberry canes were the telltale chicken tracks of a grouse headed for a lakeside stand of spruce trees. I followed them on alert, expecting a wild, whirring flush. Sage bounded in, puppy energy on display, leaping deadfalls and burrowing into the logging slash.

The grouse hadn't made it to the other side of the protective barrier of evergreens. Sage flushed it, thundering off on an escape route towards the nearest pine. I thumbed the right hammer back, the gun boomed and gunsmoke clouded out in front, blocking my view. I cocked the left hammer and hoped for a second flush while Sage searched the area. No second flush. And no retrieve. Score one for the grouse.

No more grouse showed themselves that day despite all those I had seen while deer hunting. Winter Northwoods grouse are fickle. They might be alone in logging regrowth like the missed one. They might be bunched up in big flocks in dense swamps. They might flush wildly from a tree a hundred yards out. Or they might explode from the snow inches from the dog's nose. Like December deer, most are seasoned veterans. Escapes from predators, human hunters, and weather are everyday occurrences.

Two days later, Sage and I went back to see if that grouse was still around. The weather was the same cloudy-with-a-chance-of-snowflakes. We covered the area without a flush, then moved up the shore until once again there were chicken tracks near a pine grove. I found an open area to swing the gun and let Sage do her job. This time the grouse flushed from a jack pine with a head start and the same get-behind-the-next-tree escape plan. I had to rush my shot but the gun fired and belched a thin gray cloud. Sage bounded through the thickets searching while I waited. Nothing. Again. This was starting to get personal.

I still have responsibilities at home around the holidays. It took me three weeks to take care of those and get back to the cabin for another chance at that grouse. The four-wheel drive was now working on the SUV. However, another problem had replaced that one. The percussion cap nipples had been removed from the double-barrel during cleaning back at home. That's where they still were—two-hundred miles away. I dug through all the accouterments I did bring and found one nipple. A double-barrel needs two to have both barrels operational. So I was now wandering the woods with a single-shot double-barrel.

We got right to the point and headed straight to the spruce tree clump to see if anyone was home. For a Labrador puppy, Sage is better than most. She spent the fall retrieving ducks, woodcock, grouse, and even assisted with a big Canada goose. This time she quartered ahead a bit too far and flushed the grouse from an open clear cut. A fifty-yard shot with a muzzleloader is a waste of powder and shot. I held fire and hoped for a re-flush. Most December grouse keep on moving. So did this one.

Sage and I moved on to a swamp a couple of miles away. The sun came out as we hunted, driving the air temperature up to near freezing. We found tracks again in a low-lying area with the sun beaming in.

Sage dug into an alder clump and flushed a grouse out the other side. I held fire and hoped for a clear shot. Another one thundered out, buried in the snow in front of Sage's nose. I picked a gap between trees. The grouse appeared. I swung the gun, pulled the trigger. Bark flew as an ash tree stepped in front of the grouse and took the brunt of the load.

I was speaking a few manly words about my shooting abilities and grouse as I called Sage over. She sat at my feet with her tongue hanging out while I reloaded the right barrel on my fancy single-shot, dumping in pre-made paper cartridges of powder and shot, trying with cold hands to get the ramrod down the skinny muzzle. Sage broke from my side and hit

that alder clump one more time. One more grouse
erupted out and sailed away over the wide-open swamp.
Now that would have been an easy shot.

Hit one more spot or rebuild the fire in the
cabin wood burner and sample a cold one while a steak
sizzles on the grill? That was the question running
through my mind with sunset approaching. I kept
hunting, letting Sage romp while walking through a
recent logging area devoid of cover. When we got to
the edge, she made a loop into thick stuff, working
over and under cover on her way back, looking birdy,
as we upland bird hunters say. Of course when doesn't
a Lab puppy look birdy—like they're excited and about
to flush something? This time she was. One more of
those snow-buried grouse whirred away from the base of
the stump and tried to escape down a narrow corridor
in the trees. I hesitated a moment, blotting out the
straightaway bird with the muzzle and pulled the front
trigger. This time the white cloud of smoke couldn't
hide the sight of the grouse tumbling to the snow and
Sage chasing over to claim it as hers.

The grouse had a few defects by the time I got
it back—a little shot damage and feathers missing from
puppy enthusiasm. Picture me, dressed in camouflage
and a goofy orange hat, chasing a puppy around in the
snow, while feathers fly and the empty double-barrel
leans against a tree. I'm guessing no artist is going
to paint that picture soon.

Someday

Someday

A few years ago, a friend took me to his family's vacant farm in far northern Minnesota. There wasn't any livestock roaming the overgrown pasture and only a crumbling foundation remained of the barn. But there were signs the farm had once been occupied by frugal Scandinavian farmers like the ones I grew up with over fifty years ago. Like the low head-smacking rafters in the upstairs bedrooms of the house and the outhouse, overlooking a pond, still usable even though the house had indoor plumbing. Why spend extra money for a high ceiling in a space only used for sleeping? Or demolish an outhouse that still worked fine and might be needed someday?

I walked into the cocklebur-infested and itchweed-infested grove of boxelder trees encircling the yard and found the open-air junk yard I expected. Hulks of long-dead farm equipment. Rolls of rusty, twisted barbwire. Heaps of scrap parts from tractors and plows. Parting with metal was hard for these guys. A new machine might break down. Or maybe a hunk of rusting metal might be needed to mend a broken part or to practice welding skills. All this stuff might have a use—or be worth something—someday.

I do understand this train of thought. My wife says I have saved plenty of worthless junk myself. As usual, she's probably right. In my defense, there is at least one thing I have questioned saving, even as a kid, and not just some days.

Chores were an everyday fact of life back then and probably still are for farm kids today. Holding slopping buckets of milk under calves' noses, trying to remember which of the pushy, bawling black and white horde had already drunk. Shoveling manure from calf pens and spreading fresh straw bales. Milking cows and driving tractors once you were old enough. These had a clear purpose, an outcome, and even were fun some days.

But on a rainy day, a snowy day, a slow day, or as punishment for some misdeed, we had the worst of duties. Go to the musty dark back corner of the dirt-floored machine shed. Select a warped, paint-peeling, half-rotten board from a never-shrinking pile. Pull the most obvious nails with an old claw hammer. Run the hammer up and down the board, listening and feeling for the scrape of the one last unseen nail that was always there. Stack the board in a corner. Pound the bent nails semi-flat while pounding and pinching fingers flat in the process. Drop the semi-straight nails into an old coffee can to be used somewhere, "good enough" for some mythical project someday.

The machine shed at my friend's farm was still standing. I had a hunch and walked over, unlatched the door, and stepped inside. There they were, the fruit of the hard labor of many farm kids over many years. Shelves filled with faded coffee cans brimming with used rusty nails. Still waiting for "someday."

Strange Barn Fellows

We moved to the country one summer close to forty years ago, seeking to escape the traffic noise and neighbors that came with the old rental house in town. The farmhouse was a typical 1930s story-and-a-half that needed a few updates but was clean and secluded on a gravel road half a mile from the nearest neighbor. Included with the farmhouse was an old barn with a few cattle, a chicken coop full of laying hens, and the usual handful of farm cats. The cats fended for themselves while the cattle and chickens got once-a-day visits from the farm's owner. The cats soon made peace with our Labrador retriever and friends with our toddler son.

Late that fall the farmer emptied the cattle from the barn and shifted them to his home place for the winter. Next went the chickens, off to the soup factory, or wherever laying hens past their prime disappear to. The cats mysteriously disappeared too—perhaps following their farmer or shifting to another farm site where handouts and mice where more plentiful. Two stragglers from this menagerie remained behind. A few days after the chicken flock disappeared, a lone scraggly hen appeared. I don't know how she missed getting caught up with the rest of the flock. One day she was just there, scratching in the dirt around the chicken coop, pink skin showing through spots where white feathers were missing. I had plans for the chicken coop. So the dog and I captured her after a chase around the yard and moved her to the barn under squawking protest. There she could fend for herself in the leftover hay until the farmer found time to deal with an escapee.

Soon after, and just shortly before the onset of winter, a cat appeared on the doorstep. A young, skinny gray tabby looking for handouts and friends. I moved him into the barn too, figuring the old structure would provide him shelter and old hay bales to snuggle into. There also might be some mice to supplement the kitchen leftovers that I occasionally trudged through the snow and set inside the door. I wondered about how he and the chicken would get along. Even wondered if the chicken would end up as cat food some long, cold, hungry winter night.

The trips to the barn were usually made in the dark after returning home from work and having supper. The food kept disappearing but I rarely saw the cat or the chicken and didn't take the time to hunt for them in the dark, gloomy, cobweb-infested barn. One weekend daylight trip surprised me. I opened the barn door and found the chicken and the cat resting cheek to cheek burrowed into a nest of loose hay covering the floor. They looked up in surprise and quickly separated, like a teenaged couple caught making out by snoopy parents. I laughed and reported the unlikely alliance to Marcie. As the winter progressed, they became more used to my visits and soon didn't hide the fact that they were in some sort of a relationship. Then came spring.

On a bright sunny morning, I opened the barn door and let the pair out of the confines of the barn.

They sauntered out together, like friends taking a walk in the park. The chicken looked healthy from a restful winter and plenty of table scraps, feathers regrown and fluffy white, pecking and scratching in the gravel yard at the front of the barn. The cat did not stray far from his winter companion. Sliding around the chicken, rubbing against the hen like she was the legs of a favorite human. From there they moved on, always close.

There's a lesson or two here for people who like to think deep thoughts. The cat could have ambushed the chicken in the dark of a long winter night and dined on fresh meat. Or stayed on one end of the spacious barn. Likewise the chicken could have harassed the cat during the day and found a safe roost at night. Instead they bonded, choosing warmth and companionship over combat and loneliness.

I don't remember what happened to these unlikely companions, brought together through circumstances out of their control. But wherever they disappeared to, they left behind a memory from that morning, a mental picture I haven't lost despite the decades that have passed. On a weathered wood fence rail sits a gray tabby cat and a white hen, fur touching feather, basking in the spring sun together.

Of Mice and Me

We usually have a plan for the weekend or week at the cabin. Maybe it's to tackle a big project like splitting next winter's firewood. Or maybe it's just to relax and enjoy the swimming raft, party with the neighbors, or catch a few fish. Sometimes these plans actually work out. Then again, sometimes they are derailed by the smallest of things . . .

The old four-wheeler started after sitting under cover alongside the outhouse for a couple weeks. That in itself is always a minor victory in the ongoing Northwoods struggle of man versus machine. It stayed running for the trip downhill through the woods to neighbor Marv's. There I enjoyed an hour's worth of socialization on the lakeside deck before climbing back on the green machine to rumble back uphill. That's when the trouble started. Actually, in this case, that's when the ATV wouldn't start, once again demonstrating a problem in dealing with old machines. They will often get you where you are going. But sometimes they don't get you back.

Marv and I played backwoods mechanic until admitting defeat when the battery died. I had to hike uphill through the woods to get the trailer and haul the lifeless carcass back to the cabin. I then had an adult beverage on my own deck, letting frustration ease while the battery charger did its work. Next was checking off the usual suspects in the death of a machine. The gas tank at an adequate level despite a small leak. The emergency kill switch and the gear shifter were in their proper positions. The fuse in the starter wiring looked good. Then I dug deeper, unscrewing the bolts for the air cleaner box and lifting off the lid. Here was a problem.

The local mouse tribe, the same ones I feed bird seed all year and even tolerate in the outhouse, had accessed the filter box through the air intake tube and packed it full of shredded leaves and grass. The easy part was removing all the junk and throwing it in the fire pit for starter material. Next was a call to Joe, my friendly works-for-beer-and-parts-money small engine mechanic. He recommended removal of the carburetor and delivery to him for a thorough cleaning. I asked what brand of beer he was currently drinking and got busy. First came watching several YouTube videos, then taking a deep breath and removing the carburetor one bolt, cable, and retaining pin at a time. Thus my plans for the weekend went from fishing, swimming, and socializing, to learning new mechanical skills and inventing still more colorful new words.

Mice are an everyday fact of life at the cabin. We moved into their territory over twenty years ago and haven't tried to exterminate them, a process that would be pointless given the vast expanse of surrounding forest and the army of mice living in it. They quietly steal bird seed in the dark of night alongside the flying squirrels. They scurry past feet in the outhouse, drawing screams from uninitiated visitors. They stay out of the cabin only because it is new and tightly constructed. They do occasionally leave nests between the screen door and main door just to mark their territory.

They also work together with the chipmunks and red squirrels to keep mechanics in business. My memory isn't always the best but I can remember this list of dastardly deeds besides the ATV job: Plugged the air filter of Marcie's sister's SUV with acorns and leaves. Plugged the air filter of Marcie's car with suet and birdseed. Plugged the cannon barrel with leaves and grass (yes, we have a cannon but that's another story). At least in that case the fix was easy. I just loaded some powder in the cannon and touched it off with a satisfying BOOM, spraying the woods with shredded mice bedding. I really hope one of the little creeps was in it and got the ride of a lifetime.

So far all this guerrilla warfare hasn't caused any great monetary loss. On the other hand, hours spent at the cabin are priceless. I would just as soon not spend them reading instruction manuals and watching YouTube videos on small engine repair. And the trouble is, you never know when they have been up to mischief until it's too late.

A month or so after the ATV incident, I enlisted Marcie to drive me and the small boat to the boat launch right before dark. If I got the boat in the water this evening, I could get an early start on duck hunting in the morning and then move on to the never-ending task of next year's firewood. Marcie usually waits until I get the boat out of sight before driving the trailer back to the cabin. In this case, it was a smart move.

The little six-horse motor started just fine and got me a couple hundred yards out into the lake before dying. After the usual amount of swearing while pulling the starter rope, it sputtered to life and limped the boat back to the dock. First I checked the gas tank and fuel line connections, then pulled the cover off the motor and discovered the latest sneak attack. The motor, including air intake and carburetor, were stuffed with the now familiar wad of shredded leaves and grass.

Well, there went those plans for early duck hunting in the morning. Like some well-known philosopher used to say, sort of, "Mice can sometimes cause the best laid plans of men to go asunder."

The Bear Facts

The Bear Facts

It might not have been a dark and stormy night outside the cabin, but it was a real dark mid-summer night and quiet enough until a load crash was heard through the open screen windows. I flipped on the yard flood light and stepped out onto the deck to investigate. Note to self—next time flip the light on and look out the window, then decide whether or not to step outside. Next time the source of the noise might be a rabid Sasquatch or the Northwoods version of the Chainsaw Massacre Guy.

In this case it was four or five bears in the middle of trashing bird feeders, even though the feeders were empty in an attempt to discourage such actions. I say four or five bears because it was hard to get a positive count as they circled in and out of the flood light's sphere of influence, hell-bent on mischief. One bear had already knocked over the big platform feeder only ten feet from the deck. Another ignored my shout—"Hey, you can't do that!" and brazenly ripped the flying squirrel feeder off the oak tree right in front of my bugged-out eyes. My stupid brain couldn't process the sight of this many bears, this many very brave bears, until one stood up five feet away, put his forepaws on the deck railing and appeared to beg for treats. That got me moving. I danced back inside and quickly hunted down my shotgun and a couple of shells.

Thus armed, I squeezed through a partially

opened door once more and slammed it behind me to prevent Sage from scrambling through to join the fun. More shouting had the same negative effect. The three or four grown but smallish bears kept circling the deck, in and out of the spot light, while a larger—I assume Momma bear—stayed at the edge of the woods clacking her teeth together and growling. Enough of this. I aimed the shotgun safely off into the woods at a high angle and boomed two shots off over their heads. That worked. All four or five went crashing back in the dark towards the state forest, hopefully deterred from raiding bird feeders for at least one night.

It's a jungle out there, at our cabin on the edge of the Paul Bunyan State Forest. And in that jungle live many mysterious beasts. Most of these remain heard and not seen. Wolves howl at sunset. Owls hoot like monkeys in an African jungle. Coyotes yip and yap. Foxes bark. Bobcats just lurk, leaving pictures on well-placed trail cameras. The bears aren't so laid back. If they are hungry, they will show up day or night and leave their mark.

Now let's be clear. The bears in our neck of the woods are black bears, specifically *Ursus americanus*, the American black bear and reportedly the most common bear by numbers in the world. These should not be confused with the grizzly bears found farther out west —*Ursus arctos horribilis*. Yes, the *horribilis* in that Latin scientific name stands for what you think it does. Our black bears are pretty tame creatures and relatively harmless to people and pets compared to those. Stepping out onto the deck to greet a hungry pack of grizzlies might have caused something real "horribilis" to happen to me.

Our bears seem to just like to hassle us for easy meals, take advantage of our mistakes, and keep reminding us they were here first. This started early after our purchase of the lot. The first structure I built was an outhouse that doubled as a storage shed. It's still there, still in use for both purposes. What we store in the outhouse has changed since a bear encounter the first summer. A fifty-pound bag of sunflower seed was left after a weekend visit. When we returned a couple of weeks later, the outhouse was ransacked. Life jackets, canoe paddles, shovels, and other assorted goods had been tossed aside by a bear intent on getting the seeds. Ever wonder how strong a bear is? This one ripped the reinforced half-inch plywood door off and folded it in half. Try that yourself sometime.

The next few years were pretty much bear-free, if I remember right. Then came two instances in the summer of 1999 while the cabin was under construction. Youngest son Steve, Ripley the Retriever, and I were sleeping in a camper trailer while pouring cement for the basement floor. The dog woke me at sunrise, whining in excitement, looking out the screened camper window. There, between us and the cabin, was a big old bear, sitting back on his haunches, wolfing down Ripley's dog chow. This bear liked dog food. It returned several times that day, peering out of the thick underbrush, watching our work and hoping the dog dish got refilled. We took a run into town for supplies at one point and returned to find muddy bear prints on the cabin. One on the front door and one alongside the door where it had stood and looked in through the window. Imagine peering out that window in the dark of the night and finding yourself in a scene straight out of a Northwoods horror movie.

The mere fact that there are big strong furry beasts roaming nearby can have an effect on your mind even if you know that they are pretty harmless. It is not uncommon for someone to ask for an escort to the outhouse after dark. And no one ever heads out there without a strong flashlight. But even the daylight can bring forth fears hiding in the back of one's mind.

I was walking down the shared driveway one bright morning when, up ahead, I saw one of our neighbors bent over her driveway flower garden. The dog ran ahead to greet her. Harmless enough, you'd think. But what she saw was a big black shape rapidly closing on her from the corner of an eye—possibly a rampaging bear—not an enthusiastic Labrador retriever. To make matters worse, she had seen a bear walking down her driveway earlier in the morning. Her scream was heard for many miles. Her heart hadn't stopped racing by the time I got there and apologized.

I had one more encounter with a bear that left a real mark. In this case I was bushwhacking around the perimeter of a small lake, looking for an easy spot to fish from shore. I stepped into a clearing and noticed it was carpeted with a thick patch of blueberries, ripe and inviting. I immediately thought—"Great place to meet a bear . . ." I wasn't worried about encountering a bear given the noise I had made getting to this spot—breaking brush, swatting bugs, and swearing every time my fishing rod got tangled up in the mess.

I carefully surveyed the terrain anyway, heart rate up just a bit, took a step forward to begin picking berries, and heard and felt a big "squish" under my foot. Looking down, I discovered that a bear had indeed been here before me as my hiking boot was firmly planted into a large pile of fresh blueberry bear poop. Yeah, a little bear poo on the boot is better than a few claw marks on the torso, but it's still gonna leave a stain.

Cannon Fodder

I often offer up expert advice on what I believe a true cabin should look like or have for supporting equipment. Things like natural wood siding, a real fireplace or at least a wood stove, and a lawn mower you aren't afraid to mow over stumps with. So here's a little change of pace. There is something personal experience tells me that your cabin—and mine —should not have. A cannon. That's right. Don't build, buy, barter, or otherwise procure a cannon for your cabin. Don't do what I did.

Yes, I have a cannon. At least for the time being and I still have all of my fingers and both eyes. That might only be because I'm lucky.

Some of my adoring fans have noted that I appeared to have been inspired or influenced in my writing by the famous outdoor humorist Pat McManus. However, I can't blame Mr. McManus, his assorted colorful friends, and his famous story "Poof, No Eyebrows" for the cannon and all the related problems, past and future. The blame lies with my Uncle Fred.

Fred was the only and older brother of my mother. He was also someone that I, as a budding young sportsman, looked up to. He was known for hunting and fishing, trading guns and automobiles, and in later life, for tinkering around building things from wood and/or metal. I spent many days with him and Aunt Mickey at their cabin on a western Minnesota lake. He found me my first shotgun and .22 rifle and held on to them until it was legal and parent-approved for me to possess them. So I owe a lot to Fred and thank him posthumously for all that. Now comes the cannon—the jury is still out on that.

About forty years ago Uncle Fred decided to construct a cannon, a real cannon, like back from the Civil War days. His inspiration might have been his love of firearms or something seen on TV or a hare-brained idea based on the availability of some pipe, old farm equipment parts, and his welding skills. Three different diameters of steel pipe were fitted inside each other and solidly welded together to make a barrel. The rear of the barrel was fitted with a threaded pipe cap bored out to hold a charge of powder and accept a length of cannon fuse. An old set of steel-spoked farm machinery wheels and a sturdy piece of metal rod made a wheeled carriage and there you have it—a cannon.

Now, what does an old Scandinavian tinkerer do with a cannon? I don't know if he ever shot it himself. I believe by then he was living in town and probably would not have touched it off in the back yard to impress the neighbors. All I know is that it ended up sitting on the lawn of my parent's lake home as a donation to his little sister.

Luckily by this time my two brothers and I were of somewhat responsible age—late twenties or something like that. That probably has something to do with all of us still having our fingers and toes as mentioned earlier. Had we been teenagers, well, you can probably guess what might have happened. Testosterone and gunpowder can be a dangerous mix.

Anyway, being somewhat responsible did not stop Dad and us male offspring from experimenting with it. After all, what male and maybe even a few females haven't dreamed of making a bigger noise and causing more destruction than a few Minnesota illegal fireworks? We bought some black powder, cannon fuse, and pointed our menacingly painted black cannon out over the lake. How much powder did we use? I don't know. The cannon didn't come with instructions. We just had to experiment. Projectiles? A tennis ball might fit but what fun was that? The rocky shoreline of Fox Lake was littered with stones conveniently rounded by glacial activity and waves for the last ten thousand years. Why not? It was a wide-open empty lake after all.

We loaded the cannon from behind with a small handful of powder, stuffed some newspaper in the front for wadding, and pushed a two-inch rock down the bore using an old broom handle for a ramrod. We then lit the three-inch cannon fuse and scrambled back.

The resulting boom and cloud of smoke was very satisfying—a Fourth of July noise-maker that drowned out all those competing illegal fireworks. The rock? It sailed out over the lake unseen, kept on sailing much farther than anticipated, and splashed down over a quarter of a mile away out in the middle of the once-empty lake. I'm not sure if the boat and water skier that suddenly appeared ever noticed the boom, smoke, and splash. I'm sure they would have cruised over and thanked us if they had.

Now you might think that sobering experience would have ended our experimentation. Or maybe you already know the answer. We nixed the idea of solid round projectiles and moved on to spears. A spear-chucking cannon? Hey, why not? It seemed safer than rocks for some reason. We backed off on the powder a bit for the next load, used the same old broom handle to stuff the newspaper wadding in, and then stuck a mostly straight stick down the barrel for fun.

The second boom and cloud of smoke was equally as satisfying as the first. The stick was easy to follow as it launched out over the lawn. Now I mentioned the stick was mostly straight. It's hard to find a perfectly straight stick for a spur-of-the-moment cannon shot. This one had a slight bend to the left as loaded in the cannon. Halfway across the lawn the bend effected the aerodynamics—or would that be "arrow dynamics"—and its flight path altered dramatically to the left, straight on a slow motion collision course for the windshield of the old Larson cruiser sitting on the boat lift. This disaster was averted only by inches as the spear passed just above the windshield and took a hard left into the lake by the point.

I think another water-skier came by close to shore just as this happened. Thus ended the projectile firing part of our cannon experiment. We were all in agreement that noise and smoke were fun enough.

My parents sold the lake home a few years later and downsized just about the time we became cabin owners. So it made perfect sense that I, Uncle Fred's favorite nephew and Mom's favorite son, should inherit the cannon and move it to the less-populated North Country.

So that's how I became a proud cannon owner. It

sits at the top of the hillside pointed out over the lake. We have held to that "no projectile" rule pretty good. There was one little reminder early after we moved the cannon north. As I remember, a rock ricocheted off the big pine tree in front of the cabin and caused a little excitement but no lasting damage.

We now limit cannon usage to closely supervised holiday celebrations. It is ready to ring in the New Year or commemorate the Fourth of July with a big bang, a cloud of smoke, and a video posted on social media just to prove we have a cannon. The boom reverberates down the hill and echoes back from the far side of the lake with a very satisfying rumble. I think Uncle Fred would be proud—especially since his favorite nephew, and his favorite nephew's sons, still have all their parts.

Some Nights Have Names

Nightfall away from the comforts of home is sometimes a soothing, magical time. Camping in the boondocks or lying awake at the cabin with the windows wide open while loon wails and owl hoots echo in the still air. A sense of peace and comforting hope that all is right with the world and the sun will rise again. I've had many of these nights over the years. Even ones where I was afraid to sleep for fear of missing something.

On a still sunny afternoon I four-wheeled the truck into a remote campsite along the Missouri River. This spot was farther back in the bush than a lone elk hunter should be, given the weather forecast. The bright sun was predicted to dim with two days of rain and snow, stranding me for at least four days while the muddy roads dried out. That's where the elk were, where I had to be. I had supplies, warm gear, time, and the authorities, both formal and family, had been notified of my whereabouts and plans.

A long day on the road meant an early lights out. I snuggled into a warm sleeping bag soon after dark and lay awake, planning the next day's hunt, thinking of places where an elk or two might shelter in the cold drizzle, sleet, and snow the daylight would bring. Then the show started. Elk emerged from the thick willows of the river bottoms. Others paraded down from the hills above. They converged on the clearing and got their rut on, either oblivious to my simple campsite or simply not caring under the dark of night.

Bugling. Screaming. Horn bumping. Brush thrashing. Cows calling to lost calves and prospective mates. It was all going down as they got in one last crazy hormone-fueled night of fun and games before the coming storm. I was a silent witness to one of nature's grand parties. It was only after the promised rain started to pitter-patter on the roof and the party-goers left that sleep arrived. I didn't wake until the sun rose on a dreary snow-crusted landscape.

Not all nights in remote places are that exciting or result in a deep relaxing sleep. There have been nights where sleep comes late or does not come at all. Nights where sleep is made impossible by things going bump in the night. Winter nights where the lake downhill from the cabin thumps and groans in the full moonlight, making more ice and evoking nightmares of winter monsters stalking through the forest among the creepy moon shadows. Summer nights where some animal, maybe small, maybe large, coughs and circles the campsite just beyond the bright circle of light projected by the hissing gas lantern. Memories of these nights live on to become legends. Legends with names. Legends like "The Night of the Thumper."

Many years ago, my wife and I used our first real tax return to purchase a complete camping outfit—canoe, sleeping bags, tent, stove—the whole deal. The first test of this gear was to park at a remote northern Minnesota lake access and canoe across to a primitive campsite. We spent the day playing on the

beach, catching a few trout from the canoe, and eating
and drinking well around the campfire. Then the late
evening of a far north Minnesota night came with the
hordes of giant northern mosquitoes.

Forget the mosquitoes. The tent kept them at
bay. They turned out to be the least of our problems.
Long relaxing sleeping was not an option despite the
tent and the comfortable sleeping bags. A creature
started harassing us. Running up to the tent,
threatening to crash through, rattling through the
firewood and junk left around the campfire. Then the
thumping started. Loud heavy thumping like a bear,
werewolf, or Sasquatch banging some heavy weapon,
thumping some massive object.

I will be honest. I loaded the small revolver we
brought along for pest control and spent most of the
night with the gun in one hand and a flashlight in the
other, shining the weak beam out a tent window so that
I might at least fire a close warning shot. Late in
the night I was successful. It wasn't a monster bear
or hairy Bigfoot that appeared in the flashlight beam.
Remember the movie Bambi? With the character Thumper,
the young snowshoe hare who stomped his oversized feet
on the ground? There he was. Thumper, in our campsite,
doing his thing, trying to scare us out of his
territory. Thumper lived on that night, both in
reality and legends.

Monsters need not be large to cause sleepless
nights at lonely campsites. They need only be loud,
unseen, obnoxious, or combined with fears planted deep
in our minds. Late one October I made camp at a

primitive site at the far end of a four-wheel drive road. Once again I was deep into the backcountry where other hunters feared to travel and where a cell phone was as useless as a rock. The truck topper was my bedroom, complete with warm sleeping bag and mattress. Sleep did not come easy due to many cups of road coffee and the thrill of the coming adventure, hunting in this new wild, unexplored territory.

Then the hordes came. Monsters of the night, rattling through my gear, tipping coolers, thumping against the side of the truck, scratching paint while I cowered inside. One finally made it in. While the larger critters—rats, coons, and other night monsters—were kept at bay by the sturdy sides of the truck and topper, marauding mice found cracks to invade my fortress.

Just a mouse? Try sleeping with a mouse chewing up a roll of paper towels a foot away. Try sleeping while that mouse or one of his relatives scampers across your face in the darkness. Try sleeping on a night that already has a name. Try sleeping on Halloween night, deep in the wilderness, alone, while the wild things party on.

The Eagles
Have Landed

Yearly cabin journal entries document that Crooked Lake, on the average, is usually ice-free by the middle of April. On above-average years, the ice might last another week. So it was way above average when at the beginning of May I was able to walk down to the shore, set up my spotting scope, and zero in on the wildlife spectacle unfolding on the still ice-bound surface.

It had been a below-average, very bad winter for the fish of Crooked Lake. Visible through the thin melting ice along the shore and floating up through widening cracks were winter-killed fish, mainly sunfish and bass from the looks of it. While parts of Crooked Lake are deep and clear, other parts of the lake are shallow and weedy—thick aquatic forests for most of the open-water year.

It's a healthy situation most of the time. The weeds hide and protect young game fish and minnows and provide food for the ducks, geese, and swans that hang out here in the fall. But come winter, the weeds die off, decay away and steal back some of the oxygen they contributed during the summer. There's still leftover oxygen and some half-awake plants to make a little more once freeze-up comes. This year had been different. Ice came early and snow piled up on the lake. Together they blocked sunlight from penetrating to the plants and algae that were still viable. Oxygen levels in the water dropped and the most sensitive fish turned belly up.

However, Mother Nature always tries to give out some good with the bad. Now the cleanup crew had arrived for a feast. Randomly spread across the ice, dotting the frosted surface with their black plumage, was a gathering of eagles, a flock if you would, or more technically a "convocation" for people obsessed with technical terms. I could count twenty-two of them from my vantage point. There were probably more in the little bays and behind the islands, out of sight. I zoomed the spotting scope in on individual birds, able to see feathers ruffle in the wind and beaks and talons used in squabbles with the crows and ravens. Waddling awkwardly across the ice, one would cock its head to the side, peer down a crack, and then use those beaks and talons to fish a dead fish out of the crack.

The eagles seemed better adapted to this kind of fishing than the ravens that were hanging around close by. One or two of these smaller scavengers would pick an eagle to follow. The eagle would scratch and claw a fish out of a crack, stomp it to the ice with a clawed yellow foot, and tear off chunks with that big curved beak. The ravens stayed a respectful distance away, waiting for the eagle to eat the big tasty chunks and move on to another fish. Then the scramble was on for the leftovers, picking at skeletons and heads, getting the last bites.

Such a sight would have drawn national attention forty or fifty years ago. Eagles were suffering from many years of persecution based on claims they snatched up babies and kittens along with lambs, cattle, and an assortment of game birds and animals. The less-than-environmentally-friendly pesticides in use did many in as well. Their rarity turned them into celebrities. Even a single eagle might generate a local newspaper headline or stop traffic.

I was once heading back to college, cruising up the Minnesota River Valley to the Twin Cities to pick up a couple of carless fellow students. Soaring high above, riding the up-draft from the valley was a big raptor, a black bird with a white tail and head glaring bright in the sunshine. I pulled over on the busy roadside and shot two rolls of 35mm film, hoping for just one good shot of the bird high in the sky. A few years later, other Forest Service summer employees and I waited at headquarters long after quitting time. The two-way radio had reported an exciting find from a wildlife crew. They rolled late, one guy stepping from the truck waving an eagle feather as proof they had found an active nest. We greeted them like Vikings who had just won a Super Bowl, surrounding them, shaking hands, asking for details, and touching the feather like the trophy it was.

Now, even the city dwellers have become used to eagles. They perch on power-line poles along the freeway, feast on road-killed deer at rush hour, and entertain millions at their nests via internet-linked video cameras. Here at the lake, they build nests over cabins and hang around fishing boats looking for handouts of dead minnows and rough fish.

I was recently reminded about how much they are taken for granted. At a conference at a Twin Cites nature center, a bunch of us environmental professionals were listening to an expert from California talk about the latest in electrical energy production—things like solar and wind power. She stopped in mid-sentence, gasped, and pointed out a window. "Look, there's an eagle outside!"

The crowd of local attendees looked at each other, shrugged, and waited for her to get back to the PowerPoint. She looked over the crowd, ran to the window, and again pointed outside. "I'm not kidding! There's an eagle sitting right outside the window!"

She got the same "so what" reaction from the crowd. She shook her head at our lack of interest, watched the eagle for a minute more and then turned and asked, "Do you know how good you have it here? This doesn't happen in Los Angeles."

So today I stayed awhile down at the lake, with that gathering of eagles, appreciating a conservation success story. Last year's immature youngsters, still all mottled black without white heads or tails, were interacting with their semi-interested parents and fending off the ravens for scraps. Given the number of fish being devoured, it looked like it won't be a banner fishing year on the lake. But maybe a few more of these eagles will hang around and grace us with their presence, soaring high above the lake with the turkey buzzards, fighting the resident ospreys for more fish and screeching from the tops of tall pines in the mornings. Here in the North Country you have to take the bad with the good and I'm betting there's still enough fish left in the lake for all of us.

The Sweet Stink
of Vacation

Sometimes a vacation really stinks. And I mean that in both a literal and figurative sense. Here I was, on vacation near the pristine Boundary Waters Canoe Area Wilderness, flat on my back, contorted under the rear deck of my Big Boat, arm twisted and bent, reaching far up under the boat's floor, digging in the bilge water for a three-days-dead crappie.

A dead crappie in the bilge? For three days? Sometimes these things happen. It all started with a dead battery instead of a dead fish. Batteries, especially boat batteries, often die on vacations, timing their demise to cause the most amount of disruption possible and a large unplanned purchase from carefully planned vacation funds. Then comes the hassle of installation.

Jury-rigging the new battery into the electrical system without proper tools and facilities left the sliding doors to the gas and battery compartment inoperable and thus the bilge partially exposed. But we were on vacation and the crappies were biting—the boat was needed. Son Andy held a large crappie up for his Significant Other Steph and me to admire, intending to toss it back into the lake to swim another day. A powerful flop ripped it from his grip and to the floor. One more flop and it was gone, straight into the bilge, frantically swimming upstream, far up under the floor, and far out of reach. Now, three days later, it was stinking.

I should be breathing in clean fresh air with a hint of pine trees baking in the summer sun while they shade the dock. Clean fresh air, purified by the early morning rain that had soaked the boat carpet and was now soaking through my fishing pants. Pants that smelled a little funky even before they got wet. Pants I had worn for five days straight and upon which many things had been spilled. Things like fish-fry grease, motor oil, and strong coffee with cream and maybe just a splash of brandy.

The boat had accumulated a few smells long before the crappie incident. Smells that could be smelt from my current position. The funk of spilled beer and minnow bucket water. The fishy musk of northern pike slime. Some guys don't even allow these fish in their boats since their slime coats hands, clothes, nets, and boat floor carpet as they are swung over the gunwale, twisting and flopping, sliming and smelling. For me, it's a smell straight from a childhood spent dreaming of big pike, caught on too-short summer vacations while trolling pine-scented shores with Dad. It does stink.

Tucked under the boat's steering console nearby is another source of stink, a round white foam bait container with the remains of a dozen night crawlers. Ever lifted the lid on a container of night crawlers that have been left in the sun too long? You'd remember if you did. The fragrance of a couple dozen week-old minnows forgotten in the live well is perfume by comparison. Let's call it a "stench." I would gladly deal with all of them if this stinkin' crappie could be pulled from the bilge.

The Sweet Stink of Vacation

I admit defeat, pull my arm back carefully past the fuel line and water tubes, through the maze of electrical wires and other stuff that comes together in this spot and yet somehow was navigated by the crappie in a successful escape to a certain death. I roll upright, use the side of the boat for a backrest and contemplate the stinking situation.

My feet smell from too many days in the same wet pair of shoes. My pants have that mixed aroma of all things previously mentioned. My sweaty T-shirt is stained in all the right places and giving forth the odors that come with the stains. My hands smell like the boat bilge—a combination of boat gas, stagnant water, and long-dead crappie. Yes, vacation is really beginning to stink.

I stand up, grab the red plaid sweatshirt tossed aside at the start of the bilge-fishing exercise, and step onto the dock. There the breeze carries the sweet smell of the sun-warmed pines mixed with subtle undertones of a warm summer afternoon in the forest. And the sweatshirt in my hands adds its own aromas to the mix. Woodsmoke with a hint of burnt marshmallow from last night's campfire, mixed with this morning's crispy fried bacon and blueberry pancakes. I hold it to my face and take a deep breath. That's what vacation is supposed to smell like.

Crooked Lake Chowder

Like many Lake Country residents, the roots of my family tree reach back deep into Scandinavian soil. Unfortunately, many of my family's Norwegian traditions, including ethnic cuisine, got lost somewhere in over one-hundred-fifty years of Minnesota history. My childhood memories include delicacies like sweet spritz cookies and crispy krumkaker, and my mother is still a world-class lefsa flipper. That is about where our edible traditions end. I didn't even come face-to-face with true lutefisk until I was more than forty years old.

Our Christmas meal was unique although not necessarily of true Scandinavian origin. Our extended family would gather for a supper of oyster stew with little round crackers floating in it. True to our frugal heritage, the oysters came from a can—none of those expensive fresh ones even if they were available. The idea was to have a simple, special meal with limited clean-up before the mad rush to the presents under the tree. These days oyster stew seems to be an acquired taste that the young folk and in-laws seem unwilling to acquire. Besides that, our Christmas meal, with even more extended family, has become more elaborate despite the resulting mountain of dirty dishes.

It seemed like time for a new tradition with a true Norse theme. I began searching cookbooks and the internet for options. A fish soup recipe from the famed Bergen, Norway, fish market seemed like a traditional replacement for the oyster stew. However, my first attempts to make it were less than remarkable despite using imported expensive cod and salmon straight from the Homeland. I doubted my results were capturing the true essence of fresh Scandinavian fish and seafood.

It took a two-years-late twenty-fifth wedding anniversary adventure to Iceland to show what I was missing. Marcie and I flew to Reykjavik looking for a change of pace with a Nordic flair without the time and money needed to reach the family homestead near Oslo, Norway. After spending a morning downtown rummaging through the Kolaportid flea market, feeding swans at Tjorn Lake, and climbing the Hallgrimskirkja church steeple to look across Faxafloi Bay at the Snaefellsnes Peninsula, we took a break from trying to pronounce unpronounceable names. We wandered into Laekjarbrekka, a highly recommended restaurant located in one of the oldest buildings in the city. The fish soup lunch special caught my eye.

The soup arrived in a wide flat bowl, chunks of fish, lobster, and scallops swimming in a thick creamy stock. It had more texture and variety than my weak attempts back home and a mystery background flavor that kept us guessing—and savoring—at every spoonful. When we returned home, the experiments began anew, hoping to discover the right combination of mystery ingredients. The new efforts were good, but not nearly as good as that memorable Icelandic lunch. My frustration grew until I did the obvious. I swallowed my manly pride and emailed Laekjarbrekka to ask for the recipe. A cheerful message quickly bounced back from Chef Veronika, offering preparation tips and "secret" ingredients. Who would have guessed that curry powder and cognac are traditional Scandinavian ingredients?

My first attempt was a definite flashback to Iceland. The soup got better with every attempt. I'm not saying it rivals Veronika's masterpiece but I'm not ashamed to make it for friends and family—or just a small batch to hoard all to myself.

Here's a quick basic recipe to try in the privacy of your own home before moving on to the advanced version we'll get to later.

Get out a big soup pot—I like my porcelain-coated five-quart Dutch oven. Sauté one bunch of chopped green onions and half a cup or so of baby carrot slivers in a couple tablespoons of olive oil. Add a chopped clove of garlic a minute before the onions and carrots are cooked. Add in a cup of white wine, three tablespoons of unsalted butter, and one of the secret ingredients—a quarter teaspoon of curry powder. Let that simmer for a few moments. Add two cups of fish stock or vegetable stock. I know fish stock is hard to come by in Minnesota. It can be made if you are willing to research options. That's what the internet is for.

Now comes the fun stuff. Add in about two pounds of mixed fish and shell fish. I like half a pound of scallops, half a pound of raw shrimp cut into one-inch pieces, and a pound of cod, also cut into one-inch pieces. Bring back to a simmer for around four minutes. Now add in a cup of cream and that other secret ingredient—a shot of brandy or cognac. Heat up, stirring constantly. Thicken with a tablespoon of corn starch if you want, add sea salt and fresh ground pepper to taste. ENJOY!

If you think the results have promise, start experimenting. Chef Veronika encourages that—"You should try something like that again and again and then you will have your own secret recipe!" Try other seafood including lobster if you really want the good stuff and have the budget. Also note that curry powder really varies in flavor from brand to brand—add more or less as you get a feel for the taste. Or leave it out altogether; it's your choice.

Now here's my "Minnesota Cabin Version" for those adventurous cabin cooks. I know fresh seafood might be hard to come by at the cabin, so here's some thoughts on ingredient choices. Walleye, perch, or any of those favorites can substitute for cod. Another choice is eelpout—try it, you'll like it! Northern pike probably works too—just make sure you know a "boneless" fillet method and that the fillets are thick enough to hold up in the soup. Walleye cheeks add the texture and eye appeal of scallops if you happen to have a surplus of them.

As an alternative to shrimp and/or lobster, try having the kids catch some crayfish off the dock. Let a couple dozen soak in a bucket of water overnight to clean their digestive systems out, pop them into salted, boiling water for a few minutes, and use the tail meat. It's like removing the meat from a lobster tail only on a smaller scale.

Here's another thing I've found. The idea of "fish soup" or even "seafood soup" doesn't sound appealing to many people, some of my friends and relatives included. Maybe it conjures up nasty images of fish heads swimming in a murky broth. So if your target eaters don't feel comfortable with the idea, call it a "chowder" and see what happens. The guys I cook for on our Canadian fishing trip seem okay with that.

You can even add one more secret ingredient to win them over. Add in some precooked bacon near the end. Everything's better with bacon.

August

Summer lasts just three short months in the North Country, three months that each have a theme and rhythm of their own. June is full of excitement—kids just set free from school, swimmable water temperatures at last, and sunfish once again nibbling toes off the dock. July has its national holiday and community festivals underway in every little burg, every weekend somewhere. Then comes August. The thrill of summer starts to wane as kids and parents think ahead to a new school year, and the vacation hour bank at work is all but empty. On top of that, August can be hot, muggy, and uncomfortable, even at the lake as the dog days of summer set in.

For me, it's the least hectic month of the summer and one that invites slowing down, relaxing, and taking time to find ways to enjoy the last bit of summer. The sun has started to shorten its day and in a good way. It's now possible to get up at sunrise and make a pot of coffee without waking other cabin occupants way too early. There's just enough daylight to spend an evening out on the lake, dock the boat, clean a few fish, and still have a quiet conversation around the campfire without suddenly realizing that the evening of one day has passed into the morning of another.

It's a time for a little "Me" time—or, in this case, a little "Us" time. Marcie and I, cooler and snacks in hand, follow the dogs down to the dock on Sunday evening. The usual weekend cabin company has left, the tourists from the nearby resorts are headed home. It's only us and a few resident neighbors left to enjoy the lake. The Big Boat is waiting at the dock, having spent the last month here at the lake, not languishing at home in the garage in a land where the lakes are green and uninviting this time of year. Tonight we have the comfort of adjustable padded seats, a flat floor for the dogs to roam, and the dependable start of the motor at the turn of a key, instead of the bench seats and the yanking pull-start and swearing associated with the little boat.

We idle out into the middle of the bay across still water, the bow parting reflections of trees and clouds, sending them rippling to the side. Neighbor Marv has the same idea. His gold and brown boat is the only other in sight. The lake is his and ours, at least for tonight. We exchange the usual pleasantries and fishing info. The dogs stand at the rail of the boat, tails wagging, hoping Marv will toss a treat across the gap between us. Then we slowly drift apart, each boat on its own mission of solitude.

Marv and I will fish tonight, or at least we will have a line dangling overboard, just in case the boat happens to drift over that mythical school of summer crappies, suspended halfway down in the cool water. But along with the quiet time and solitude will come the main attraction: a celestial show of the moon, the stars, and meteors converging on a still summer night.

The moon is the first arrival, a near-full gold disk making an appearance over the eastern horizon a full hour before the sun sets into the trees to the west. It grows in brilliance as the sunlight fades, spreading a trail of sparkling diamond highlights along its reflection on the dark water. It tries to drown out the stars with this brilliance but here, in the clear skies of lake country, they shine on determined to not be outdone. They are the warm-up acts; the real star of the show comes on stage soon. Sage sprawls out on the front deck, tired from an afternoon of fetching tennis balls off the dock. Marcie pulls Kaffi up into her lap for a cuddle. We lean back watching the sky for the fireworks to begin.

It's not some lawless neighbor's fireworks display we are watching for tonight. A much more natural, quiet display is about to begin. The Perseids meteor shower visits the skies in our neck of the woods from late July to late August. It varies from day to day, year to year, but experts claim that in mid-August it's possible to see fifty or more meteors per hour, on a clear night, with a little luck. More some years if you are willing to stay up well into the dark of the next day. For those with inquiring minds, the Perseids are named because they appear in the sky near the Perseus constellation of stars. They actually originated as particles released from the Swift-Tuttle comet.

Let's put science aside tonight and just enjoy the show. I drop the electric motor down off the bow and sit back in my own Captain's chair, occasionally bumping the foot control to keep the boat facing north. We float the dark water in the middle of the bay, suspended under the dome of the sky, real stars and their reflections surrounding us. Just us, adrift in our own private and natural planetarium, with the moon, the stars, and the streak of the first meteor of a perfect August night.